Cover design: Christopher Doll
Published By: Vagabond Publishing
Printed in the United States of America

Anton Meyers was watching the display on his desk, nervously rubbing a finger over his upper lip. The Guild took control of Aldrin dome a few weeks earlier, when the Coalition administrator failed to do anything to help people stricken by the bombing attacks that had occurred. He then approved operations to scout and clear the almost deserted Armstrong dome in preparation for expanding the Transport Guild's influence to both domes on Luna's surface. He was still a little shocked at how well things seemed to be going, with their nascent militia working to restore order and engineering teams getting the systems in the mostly abandoned Syndicate dome operational ahead of schedule.

Now he was waiting to discover the results of an even more ambitious project. The kind that could either solidify support behind the Guild, or turn the system away from them completely. He'd discussed the plan with captains of the Guild freighters at length. There were fourteen ships remaining in their small fleet, providing fourteen voices with differing opinions when they met with the president of their Guild. Not surprisingly, several of those voices had been against the proposed operation, but most showed support.

Captain Frost, on the *Vagabond*, was one of those who were enthusiastic about the idea. His opinion was becoming more respected, as the other captains observed his many actions in the fight against the Syndicate cruiser that threatened to wipe away anyone with differing views from those of the ruling Executive Committee. Frost's approval had swayed a few others who were uncertain, until even those not in agreement bowed to the will of the group.

Meyers was no fool, however. He kept those dissenting voices foremost in his thoughts, and retained their ships in orbit around Luna when the action started. Ostensibly, to provide a defensive screen in case the Syndicate decided to send the *Indomitable* their direction when they saw an opportunity to reduce an already minimal threat. He also worried about the Coalition reaction, but with that government having lost their fleet he wasn't concerned for any retaliatory actions in the near future. The only Coalition frigate left, *Waterloo*, was currently in orbit around Luna and working alongside the Guild.

The Coalition government, led by a prime minister in his third and constitutionally final term, had responded to sudden Syndicate aggression slowly. In the beginning, Meyers thought perhaps they were too locked into stagnation after twenty years of cold war. But now, a growing suspicion that the prime minister was actively sabotaging his own government in exchange for some kind of payoff from the ultra rich leaders of the corporate Syndicate had been all but confirmed. Bomb fragments found while clearing the transit tunnel between Aldrin and Armstrong had revealed the device to be a Coalition Marine explosive that was tightly controlled. DNA samples found inside the casing pointed the finger squarely at a new minister high in the government. Theodore Poul, Minister of Propaganda.

Even before that proof was found, Meyers had shared his growing suspicions and the reasoning behind them with the Minister of Defense, Rinde Brighton. During their video conference, the connection had been severed and he'd been unable to get in contact with Rinde again. It had taken several days, but he finally got word from agents on the ground that the Defense Minister had been arrested on charges of treason and sent to a factory complex that served as a work camp for political dissidents and journalists who'd tried to publish the wrong stories. It was a place that Meyers had discovered a few weeks earlier during his research into the prime minister. A dark hole that people disappeared into without trial or a chance to state their case.

The door to his office opened, the only walled-off space in the Guildhall that had served as the administrative heart of the Transport Guild for their twenty year existence. The hubbub and clamor from the dozens of desks crammed into the wide open area filled the room before the woman entering pulled the door shut behind her. Dexterity Avila, more mature than her twenty five years would lead you to believe, had risen to become the vice president of the Guild and the person Meyers leaned on most.

"Any news yet?" she asked, walking over to the small desk on the opposite side of the room. He'd had it brought in, along with secure server cabinets and other things Dex needed to do her job, when he realized the days of the Guild being a collection of simple freighters carrying cargo from one place to another were over. Events were pushing them to become something more.

"No, not since they began their descent." Meyers turned his eyes back to the holo display floating in the air at eye level.

"It hasn't been that long. I'm sure we'll hear something soon."

Even as Dex was speaking, the display flashed with a connection request. Meyers stabbed at the screen, accepting and sending the feed over to the main display on the wall that he and Dex could both see. The face that appeared on the screen was a familiar one after the events of the last year. Youthful, only a year older than Dex, framed by wild dark blonde hair with startling blue eyes gazing into the camera. Erik Frost was smiling, a mixture of triumph and joy. "We got them," he said simply.

Meyers slumped in relief, releasing all the tension he'd been carrying since giving the orders to start the rescue operation. "Did you encounter any difficulties?"

"No, sir. The first groups of factory workers were waiting on the tarmac as you expected. One of the agents with the group that boarded reports that guards have been putting up resistance, but none of them expected prisoners to fight back after so many years of drudgery and depression. They got complacent."

"In this case, complacency is good. I want to rescue every one of those poor souls." Meyers glanced at his display again, noting the approach of the freighter and their estimated time of landing at the Aldrin docking facility. "How is our special guest doing?"

"Very well. He took the opportunity to clean up and change into the suit you provided. He's in the cargo bay now, checking on the others and making sure they have the food and water they need after so much deprivation."

Meyers smiled in admiration. "Yes, I would expect nothing less. It's that compassion and concern that makes him the ideal candidate. Safe travels, Erik. We'll meet you at the docks when you land."

The screen went black, and he glanced at Dexterity to see a radiant smile on her lips. He knew only part of that was from the success of the first stage of the operation. The rest would be from seeing the man she loved, and knowing he was safe. "Is everything ready for their arrival, Dex?"

She turned toward him, blushing slightly when she saw his knowing grin. "Yes, sir. We'll have everything set up and ready to go as soon as the *Vagabond* is on the ground."

"Excellent work, as always. We have a couple of hours, so let's run through everything one more time. I want this to go smoothly. After all, this is going to be make or break for the Guild. If we fall flat on our face from the starting gate, no one will take us seriously going forward."

On the way to the recently repaired and expanded docking facility a few hours later, Meyers took time to stop in the central square. A fifth militia squad had recently been formed with the latest recruits, and Captain Fitz was running them through the early stages of their training. Tom Fitz had been a crew member on the freighter *Telemachus* eight years earlier, when that ship had taken a shipment to what had been called a "black site". It turned out to be the Syndicate cruiser, in the early stages of construction, and the crew had broken the restrictions against getting a view of their destination. After seven years spent on the *Indomitable*, first as a prisoner and then as a reluctant Marine grunt, Tom and a couple of others had aided in the escape of the *Vagabond*. Now, he was putting those years of Marine training to use, leading the newly formed militia.

The militia captain noticed Meyers watching, and offered a nod before turning to bark at one of the recruits who had stumbled through the exercise. Meyers had offered the job to Tom on impulse after he returned on the *Vagabond*, but it had proven to be an excellent decision. Even the earliest militia recruits, jaded veterans of the Coalition and Syndicate Marines and ground forces, had come to respect Captain Fitz and accept his command.

Beyond the men and women in training, he could see the dome administration building. It was empty now, with the last of the Coalition government workers having fled to Earth once the docking facility was repaired from the bombings. The building was taped off, with two militia guards on patrol around it at all times to keep any looters or curious explorers away. Meyers knew he'd have to make a decision soon on what to do with it. The Guildhall was bursting at the seams, and he could use the extra space for his growing organization.

Dex exited the Guildhall, staring down at the tablet she always carried to continue her work whenever she was walking somewhere. He snorted in amusement, wondering if he'd need to force her to get an assistant to take some of that work off her plate. She might need two, if things worked out as he hoped.

"Everyone is ready at the docking facility," she told him. "We have stations set up to process the new arrivals, and I managed to get eight of our representatives off the desks to escort our arrivals to their new homes in Armstrong." She raised her head long enough to glance toward the transit tunnel. A second bombing had caved it in, killing two thirds of the Coalition Marines in the process, but it was now cleared and operational once more.

Armstrong dome had been victim to a bomb, as well. A massive explosion that had scooped a crater out of the central square and damaged the life support equipment. The Syndicate Marines and administration had fled, along with the most important citizens, leaving the other survivors to fend for themselves. By the time Meyers was able to send in scouting teams, very few of them were left. One of those survivors, a man named Cullen who had served as a Marine years before, now worked alongside Captain Fitz with the militia.

Once the dome was reclaimed, teams of engineers had repaired the reactor and life support functions. Groups of volunteers still worked to prepare the surviving buildings to accept new residents, while also clearing the debris left from the bombing. It was work that would take months to complete, if not years, and Meyers knew he couldn't devote too many resources to it with other projects in the works that were of greater importance.

As soon as the freighter touched down on one of the two rebuilt docking pads, Meyers and Dex were standing near the airlock. Nervousness and impatience battled within him. Nervousness that their most important guest wouldn't be receptive to his ideas, and impatience to get started on work that he felt would set the system back on its feet. It was a relief when the airlock began to hiss as the door slowly opened.

The first man to step through was tall and gaunt after the stress and deprivation of the previous weeks. His tightly cut black hair was going gray almost as fast as Meyers' own, but his dark skin still showed only a handful of wrinkles. His brown eyes were alert and inquisitive, darting all around the docking facility before landing on the two people waiting to greet him.

Meyers stepped forward with a genuine smile of welcome, raising a hand to grasp the other man's in a firm handshake. "Rinde! You don't know how good it is to see your face again."

"No better than it is to see yours, my friend." The man's voice was deep, with a strong accent of his native Lagos. It was the city he had been born in, and the place his political career started before he got elected to join the Coalition Parliament and rose to become the Minister of Defense. "I thank you with all my heart for your help in releasing us from that horrible place."

"If I'd known such a thing as the factory existed, I wouldn't have waited as long as I did." Meyers examined him, one hand tightly clenched on his shoulder. "How do you feel, Rinde? Are you strong enough to help me start a revolution?"

Rinde stared at him for a moment, with a searching gaze. "If it will help us to rid the people of the prime minister's corrupt leadership, then I will give you my full support."

Meyers chuckled, ushering the man out of the way as other rescued factory workers exited the airlock. They looked around in wonder as Guild representatives hurried forward to point them to the waiting stations where details such as names and biometrics would be entered into the Aldrin servers. Then the new arrivals would be escorted to Armstrong, shown to temporary homes.

"Rinde, you and I both know that the prime minister has done everything he could to remove any opposition. Those who weren't killed in the bombings will be found among your fellow factory workers. It will take us days to get everyone off the surface, but once we do I feel confident we'll have enough people to form a government. A rightful government for the people of the Coalition."

"But we will not be an elected government, President Meyers." Rinde raised his head, adamant on this point. "Without elections, any government you form will be even less legitimate than that of our prime minister."

"Perhaps, but would you rather we do nothing and let the Syndicate take control of the entire planet?" Meyers kept his voice low, not wanting those passing nearby to hear their discussion. "That's what your prime minister wants, to sell his nation to the Syndicate leaders. To take away the freedoms that the Coalition constitution demands and protects."

Rinde grimaced, recognizing the truth in the words. "I will not make this decision on my own," he said at last. "Let us see who is rescued from the factory, and then we will all discuss this idea and come to a consensus."

"Fair enough," Meyers said, feeling frustrated but understanding the cautious approach. It also made sense to his political nature, knowing that a strong backing of support would go a long way to helping legitimize a competing government. "I've set you up with a home here in Aldrin. Dex can show you the way if you're ready."

The minister raised an eyebrow, glancing over to the lines forming at the processing stations. "I will have no special treatment, President Meyers. If there is one thing I have learned in these last few months, it is that we must experience the same things as those we claim to represent. I will stand in line with my people, and then I will live among them."

Meyers sighed, but nodded in agreement. "Very well. Dex, have Minister Brighton's quarters reset. We'll have the processors assign him a random location in Armstrong." She was already working on it as he spoke, fingers flying across the screen of the tablet. "Rinde, I'll let you get settled in. How about we meet tomorrow morning? I'll have someone escort you to the Guildhall."

Two

The *Vagabond* was completing her third trip to the planet when Erik saw a shuttle burn quickly from the Syndicate orbital station to the *Indomitable*. He knew the look of a supply shuttle well, and briefly wondered what was being carried to the cruiser from the station. There wasn't much time for the thought, however, as Mira alerted him to their arrival.

"We're down, cap. Making connection with the tube now, if you want to show our guests to the exit."

"I know they'll be glad to get out of the cargo bay. It looks like a sardine can in there." He checked the status of the rescue operations, and flipped on the ship's comms. "Three hour break after this offload, folks. We're seven back in the queue for another drop to the factory."

He made his way to the cargo bay quickly, amused to see that once again the evacuees had put themselves into variously sized groupings. As before, a small group near the door were the accepted leaders. They watched him with caution as he approached.

"We've arrived at Aldrin dome on Luna." He spoke to the leaders, but loudly enough for most of the others to hear him, as well. "Six people at a time will exit through the airlocks, so the unloading process may take as long as half an hour. Once you arrive in the docking facility, you'll be met by Guild representatives. They'll speak with you about what to expect in the days to come, and where you'll live. Armstrong dome's life support systems are repaired, and everyone will receive quarters there."

Erik paused, waiting out the ripple that passed through the crowd as those in the middle passed his words further back. "The Transport Guild is in full control of Aldrin and Armstrong. You don't need to worry about the Coalition coming after you. None of you will be returning to that factory as long as you're on Luna. If you do choose to return to Earth, that option will be made available to you in the weeks to come. We can't guarantee your safety at that point, of course."

His words created another stir in the crowd, and the murmuring voices swelled. He kept his eyes on the group leaders, and then motioned to the corridor. "Follow me, and we'll get the first group into the airlock."

Jen and Mira helped him herd the rescued factory workers through the airlocks. After each group, they had to wait at least a minute so the Guild reps on the other side had time to greet the incoming group and send them to an available desk. There, each person would be given a housing assignment, where food and some supplies would be waiting for them. Erik hadn't been sure the process would run smoothly when Dex explained it to him, but the efficiency of the Guild had prevented any issues so far.

"Hey, cap," Mira shouted from the hallway as he was ushering the next group into the ship's airlock. "The big speech is about to start. Want me to throw it up on all the screens?"

"Yeah, I want to see this, and I think our guests will find it interesting."

The airlock antechamber had three displays, two of them set above average head height to be more visible in the event of an emergency on the ship. Each of them lit up and showed an empty podium. A banner was hanging behind it, showing an unfamiliar design. A dark gray circle, representing Luna, was set in the middle of a white field, with a red circle around it for Mars. In a semi-circle above were five red stars, one for each of the mining colonies in the asteroid belt.

Several seconds later, a man in a black suit stepped behind the podium. His eyes looked into the camera, tired but full of energy. A brief bit of music blared from the speakers, causing everyone in the antechamber to turn their attention to the screen. Erik knew that those in the hallways would be looking at displays there, as well. He peered through the tiny airlock windows and saw that all activity in the docking facility had ceased, with everyone looking at nearby screens. Meyers had managed to infiltrate people into the major Earth news networks, ensuring this feed would be broadcast around the planet.

"Good morning. I am Rinde Brighton, formerly the Minister of Defense for the Coalition cabinet. I speak to you from Aldrin on Luna with a heavy heart, but with important information that every citizen of Earth, Luna, and the rest of the system has a right to know."

The inner airlock door cycled open, waiting for the next group. No one shuffled forward, too intent on the speech playing out on the displays. Brighton was laying out the evidence they had uncovered about at least one member of the prime minister's inner circle being involved in the bombings on Luna. He moved on to the prime minister's lack of response to Syndicate aggression, and a smaller box appeared on the screen displaying documents that had been obtained showing funds from a high ranking Syndicate committee member arriving in an account held in Monaco under the name of the prime minister's wife.

When Brighton started detailing the factory and the political prisoners being detained there illegally, the line of people in the antechamber and corridor let out a ragged cheer. Erik could imagine how happy they must feel to have someone speak out about the conditions and abuses they had endured. Each of them would have family on Earth wondering what had happened to them and if they were still alive.

"In light of these actions and discoveries, I am forming a Coalition splinter government on Luna. We are working in conjunction with the Colonial Alliance, formerly the Transport Guild, who are now managing affairs for Luna, Mars, and the mining colonies."

Brighton paused, looking into the camera with kind eyes. "I urge everyone on Earth to ask questions about your government. Is it still acting in your interests, or are they lining their pockets and betraying all they're supposed to stand for? Ministers and members of Parliament, if you find your conscience won't allow you to continue supporting the corrupt policies of your prime minister, there is a place for you here. It is my hope that a just government can be restored within a few months, and new elections held so our people can choose leaders who will work in their interest once more."

Rinde focused on the camera, his expression grave. "Mr. Prime Minister, if you care anything for your people, do the right thing and step down. Let us work to rebuild the government and begin to fight back against Syndicate aggression."

The displays went dark. There was half a minute of silence as everyone digested what they'd heard, and then a murmuring began to spread through the rescued factory workers in the airlock antechamber. Erik heard a lot of questions about the timeline of events laid out around the bombings. Many of these people had been so isolated in the factory that they'd only just learned about them.

Erik gently herded another group of people into the airlock, seeing the Guild representatives in the docking facility back at work after Brighton's speech. *Colonial Alliance reps*, he reminded himself. It was going to take a while to get used to the new name. Longer to adjust to the fact that he was now part of an official government.

President Meyers had presented the idea to the freighter captains late the day before, asking them to become the first fleet of the new Alliance. The administrators of the five colonies had also been on the video conference, along with a disgruntled lead scientist from Mars. The red planet was populated purely by Syndicate citizens after the *Indomitable*'s atrocities had eradicated all Coalition presence, but the scientists there had been as appalled by the actions as everyone else. Two captains had declined to become a part of the new organization. Their ships had been among those still in orbit when the Aldrin docks were destroyed, and they were unarmed freighters. Meyers had been disappointed, but accepted their resignations. All others had agreed to the proposal, and joined the Alliance fleet.

As he watched the last of the rescued people exit the *Vagabond*'s airlock, Erik took a deep breath and shared a look with Mira and Jen. The crew had discussed the changes to the Guild during the hours they waited for their third landing on Earth. He'd been surprised that the rest of the crew accepted the idea with ease. Fynn had even grumbled that it was about time. After watching the speech from Brighton, now officially Prime Minister Brighton, he'd wondered if they would feel differently.

Mira had her normal snarky grin, an expression that he'd come to find comforting no matter what situation they found themselves in. Jen merely shrugged and turned to head back to her medical bay.

"Cargo is scheduled to be loaded in fifteen," Mira said as she also left the antechamber. "Lots more food and water for our next few rounds of passengers."

Erik looked around the room, reassuring himself that nothing had been left behind by one of the evacuees. It felt good to be helping so many people, though he wondered how many would risk trying to resume their lives back on Earth. Shutting down the horrendous factory run on the labor of undocumented political prisoners was a good thing, but he didn't know how easy it would be to get their families off the planet if they were asked to do so. If the prime minister wasn't forced out of office, the man could easily arrest those family members and charge them with complicity in the action.

"Worry about now, and let later work itself out," he whispered, heading for the cargo bay to supervise the loading of fifty containers and the removal of thirty others that were empty. He needed to get the haulers in and out as quickly as possible so that the next ship could land without too much time spent in orbit.

Vagabond could hold forty evacuees on each trip, and some freighters could only manage to stuff in twenty. Even with nine of the vessels working on the rescue, it would take many days to complete the process. So far, they'd been lucky that the Coalition hadn't sent in troops to try and stop the attempt. Erik wondered if that might change now, with the announcement that those who had been held in the factory were forming a competing government.

Armstrong was going to be overtaxed by the end of it. The dome had been built to hold a thousand people, and the bomb that cratered the central square had destroyed many of the buildings in the central area. The evacuees from the factory would be forced to share homes, and overflow would eventually fill any empty spaces in Aldrin. For now, the people seemed willing to put up with the hardship, but it was going to present a serious strain on their resources.

An hour after landing, Mira was taking the *Vagabond* back into orbit again. Erik was ready for a long wait there, until the ships ahead of him had completed their drops to Earth and deliveries of human cargo to Luna. He knew that it would be at least four hours before they began their next approach to Earth. Only one ship was waiting in Earth orbit at a time, preventing ground based attacks from having a larger target of opportunity. Especially since the freighters didn't have small caliber defense cannons to shoot down incoming missiles, unlike frigates and the Syndicate cruiser. They had to rely on speed and maneuverability if they were targeted.

During the break, he headed to the galley to get a quick meal. Jen and Isaac were at the table, sitting close and laughing as they talked. Erik had to grin when he saw them, glad that the prickly doctor and shy computer tech had managed to find love in the midst of everything they'd been through. Once his heated meal was ready, he left them alone and headed to his cabin to enjoy the food.

As soon as he sat down at the small desk beside his bunk, the display pinged to alert him to an incoming call. Blowing on a forkful of steaming noodles, he pressed a few buttons to accept the connection. Dex appeared on the screen, her black curls loose as she lounged in her apartment on Luna.

"Hi, sweetie. Just wanted to check in on my favorite captain."

"He's taking a break and well deserved rest," Erik said, taking a bite of his food.

"So I see. Eating my favorite lo mein dish without me, too."

"Trust me, it's nowhere near as good as that noodle shop near the Guildhall. I'd much rather be sharing a meal with you there."

"Alliance headquarters," Dex said with a grin.

"Sorry, it's going to take me a while to get used to the change." Erik chuckled at the thought. "I never thought I'd be part of something like a government for Luna and the colonies. It feels a little surreal when I think about it too much."

She winked at him. "Wait until you find out that you're now the captain of the flagship of a fleet."

Erik choked on the noodles he was swallowing, coughing as he fumbled to grab his water pouch. "Flagship? When did that happen? Why *Vagabond*?"

Dex shook her head with laughing exasperation. "Sweetie, your ship has the fusion reactor and two heavy railguns. You're both the most advanced and most heavily armed freighter in our small fleet. Why wouldn't you be the flagship?"

He was stunned at the thought. Even during his stint on Coalition frigates, he'd never fantasized about being in charge of a fleet flagship. It added another level of pride to being a captain, but also piled on a few extra layers of responsibility. How would the older freighter captains handle him being put in a position of nominal leadership? The Alliance was still a brand new entity, with everyone having to adjust to changes in the way things were done.

Dex talked about other items she and Meyers were working on, even if she had to be vague on a few to protect secrets. He tried to give her his full attention, but kept getting lost in thoughts of his new position. By the time they'd talked for most of an hour, he had come up with dozens of things he'd like to change on his ship and across the fleet of freighters. He'd have to remember to ask Meyers about them the next time he spoke with the Alliance President.

THREE

Commander Leona Vegley was pacing the corridor. Every few steps she would glance down at her tablet to see if the message she was waiting for had arrived. She was sighing with impatience every time it wasn't there, and knew that the other officers standing along the wall of the corridor were trading glances behind her back. This was something she'd been waiting on for days, though, and she wanted to get started.

Finally, her tablet pinged and she jerked her head down to look at the screen. *Shuttle on approach*, the simple message said. She felt relief flood through her body, and went down the row of officers to make sure each of them presented a professional image. Every uniform was freshly sanitized, and aside from a few bits of lint she could find no fault.

Satisfied with the dozen people sharing the corridor, Vegley took a deep breath and marched toward the nearby entry to Bay Two. It was the place that handled the majority of the incoming cargo for the cruiser, and one of the largest on the ship. The vast compartment they entered was seven decks tall and had enough open deck space to land a couple of Guild freighters. Not that those ships would ever be allowed to get this close.

A battered cargo shuttle, one of the largest in operation from the planet below, had already passed through the ion screen that held back the vacuum of space. As Vegley was getting her ducklings into a neat row, she heard puffs of air behind her as the shuttle settled onto extended landing struts. She turned to face the blackened and scratched ship, her spine ramrod straight and chin high.

The seams of the door were visible even before it began to drop with a hydraulic whine. The hidden hinges were in obvious need of attention, as the door jerked and shuddered a few times before it made contact with the deck. The inside of the door formed a short ramp for any passengers exiting the ship. She watched the dark entry anxiously, counting the seconds until a man appeared there. He was short, but had a commanding presence that made you feel as if he were six feet tall. Close to fifty years old, his black hair was full and devoid of any gray. His Asiatic features were still smooth and unwrinkled, evidence of a life spent aboard ships and away from solar radiation. His dark eyes were alert, roaming the bay until they came to rest on the row of officers.

Vegley took a step forward, raising her arm in a salute. She could hear the officers behind her performing the same gesture, as they welcomed their admiral back to the ship. She'd been working with him for the last two days, planning out this return. After several weeks serving under the most incompetent captain she'd ever known, Vegley was more than willing to risk the consequences of going against Executive Committee orders.

Admiral Yumata walked slowly down the ramp, his gaze running across each of the officers behind her. She knew he was pleased to see every department head represented, evidence that the entire ship was behind his return to the *Indomitable*. He came to a stop at the bottom of the ramp, a slight smile playing across his thin lips. He raised his hand to return their salute.

"Welcome aboard, admiral," Vegley said as she lowered her hand. "I can't tell you how glad we are to have you back."

"It feels good to come back home," Yumata said. "Is everyone here aware of the consequences if this fails?"

"They are, admiral. *We* are."

His eyes ran across the row of officers, as if looking for any doubts or uncertainties. Finding none, he nodded sharply. "Excellent. Then let us begin."

At that moment, another man at the top of the ramp let out an angry shout. He was young, in his mid-thirties, wearing an expensive suit and haircut. A glint of gold was visible around his wrist when he raised his arm to point at them. "What the hell is going on here, Yumata? Why are these people acting like you're the man in charge? This is a problem resolution trip, nothing more."

Vegley furrowed her brow as she looked at the foppish man. She knew he was a member of the Military Committee, one of the most powerful of the Syndicate's ruling committees. He wasn't supposed to be on the shuttle, and definitely not on the cruiser. She looked to the admiral with a silent question.

Yumata raised a hand toward a squad of Marines gathered nearby. "Soldiers, take this man into custody. Make sure he doesn't leave the shuttle unless you hear from me."

"Yes, admiral," the squad sergeant said. He motioned for his soldiers, and the eight of them marched toward the shuttle and up the ramp. The committee member was screaming at them to release him, threatening their jobs when he got back to Earth, and shouting at Yumata that he would never be allowed back on the committee after such an egregious violation of his orders.

"Sorry to hear that you'll no longer be a member of the Military Committee, sir." Vegley offered a smirk with her words.

"I shall try to live with the disappointment, commander." Yumata stepped off the shuttle's ramp, turning to look back at the pilot who had appeared in the doorway with a confused look on his face. The man was looking inside the shuttle, watching the Marines restrain the committee member. "Ah," the admiral said. "Have someone unload this shuttle, commander. I have several crates on board that we will require."

Vegley turned to motion at the officer in charge of the cruiser's shipping and cargo, sending her off to complete the admiral's request. Yumata was already walking toward the exit, and she hurried to walk beside him as the rest of the department heads followed in their wake. "Tell me about Guildersen," he said.

"Admiral, Captain Guildersen has been treating this ship like his own personal fiefdom since you left us. The man barks orders that are often incomprehensible, sets deadlines that are impossible to meet, and then hands out harsh punishments to any and all at the drop of a hat." She bit her lip, thinking of the things she'd witnessed over the previous weeks. "To top it off, he's had more than a dozen people ejected from airlocks. Killed them, admiral, and I'm not entirely sure he wasn't doing it just for the joy of watching them die."

Yumata's expression was tight, his lips compressed to a thin slash across his face. The man was inscrutable at the best of times, but Vegley felt she could sense anger radiating from him. "Guildersen wasn't a good candidate for command, as I pointed out several times in annual reports to the Military Committee. His influence on the Executive Committee was too strong, even if someone did bother to read my words."

The group crowded into a lift, and Vegley punched the button for a deck high in the ship. The tight space was filled with nervous tension, and she looked around at the officers standing behind the admiral. Most had firm expressions, resolute with the decision they had all made together, but a few were looking uncertain. She wondered if any of them regretted it, now that they were so close to the end.

The lift emitted a quiet ding as it arrived at the desired deck. The doors slid open to reveal a short corridor. At the end, the corridor curved to the left to lead to quarters occupied by the highest ranking officer on board the ship. A wide door was at straight ahead, flanked by two Marines holding flechette rifles. They gawped at the group of officers exiting the lift, sharing a glance as if unsure of what to do.

Admiral Yumata strode toward the doors without hesitation, stopping only when he was a few feet away. He stood there in silence for long moments, as the Marines tried to figure out what they should do. Vegley recognized them as part of the squad that Guildersen had attached to himself and corrupted into his lackeys. She knew their first instinct had to be to call their sergeant and ask for orders on how to handle the situation.

"Marines!" she bellowed. "You will open those doors for the admiral. Now!"

She saw one of them gulp, while the other hurried to comply with the order. He slapped the panel that read his biometric information and released the locks on the door.

They slid aside silently, admitting the group onto the *Indomitable*'s command deck.

Guildersen was standing at the railing, sneering down at the people working on the main bridge below. "Ensign, if your group can't work faster than that you will be reporting to my office for punishment at the end of your shift. That would be your third time, wouldn't it? Do you know what happens the third time I have to punish one of you useless fools?"

"No," Yumata said quietly, stopping a few feet behind his former XO. "What exactly happens, Cyrus?"

That fat man whirled in surprise, moving with more grace than someone so large should possess. "What? How? You were supposed to never leave the docking bay," he spluttered.

Yumata didn't offer an answer, instead turning to look at the senior officers manning stations on the command deck. He spoke a greeting, and then stepped around Guildersen's bulk to approach the railing and look over the bridge. There were gasps of surprise, and a few shouts of joy to see their old leader returned.

Guildersen followed the movement with his beady eyes, then turned to look at the group of officers who had followed the admiral onto the command deck. "Vegley. I should have known you'd be involved in something like this. You just made your last mistake, commander. Enjoy that title for the few minutes you retain it." He shifted his gaze to the Marines standing in the open doorway. "Arrest these officers on charges of insubordination and mutiny. Transport them to airlock seventeen, and I will meet you there shortly."

"Belay that," Yumata said, not turning away from the bridge. "Arrest Mr. Guildersen for gross negligence and failure to comport himself as an officer of the fleet."

The captain gurgled a laugh. "You have overstepped yourself too far this time, Yumata. *Indomitable* is my ship, and you no longer have any authority here. Marines, send in another squad to arrest the admiral, as well. We will return him to Earth to face the Executive Committee." The gloating expression on his face was enough to make Vegley want to punch him. She was already participating in a mutiny, what did she have to lose?

Before she act on her desire, Marines brushed by her. Two of them stepped up next to Guildersen, and without a word grabbed his arms. The captain let out a surprised squawk as the Marines twisted his arms behind his back, getting his wrists as close together as possible before snapping restraints around them. Vegley turned to see the remainder of the Marine squad standing in the corridor, with the two door guards trying to stay out of their view. It was the same squad that had been waiting in the cargo bay, and returned the committee member to the shuttle.

"Thank you, sergeant." Yumata turned at last, to stare at his former first officer as the large man struggled against the soldiers. "Take Mr. Guildersen to the shuttle to wait with Mr. Abernathy. We will send them home shortly."

"Yes, admiral," one of the marines said. Both of them yanked hard on Guildersen's arm, generating a cry of pain and rage.

"You can't do this!" he screamed in a voice pitched high with fear. "I am the captain of this ship, and you will obey me. Commander, I will forgive your mutinous actions if you end this charade now. I am ordering you to release me this instant!" His words were cut off as the doors to the command deck closed. Vegley couldn't keep the grin from her face as she imagined what the fat bastard would be going through.

Yumata stepped forward to face the senior officers who had followed him from the cargo bay, as well as those still sitting at stations on the command deck. "It is an honor to return to this great ship. I hope that we can work together in the days and weeks to come to restore the *Indomitable* to her full glory. Commander, the first thing we need to do is get started on repairing our railguns and torpedo launchers. I believe we have everything we need waiting in the cargo bays?"

"Yes, admiral. The new railguns and torpedo tubes are in Cargo Bay One. I will make sure the crews get started on the work today."

"Excellent. Ladies and gentlemen, return to your departments. I will be meeting with each of you in the days to come so we can discuss how to get your individual sections working at a high level once again."

The officers saluted and left the command deck, Vegley following behind. It had been less than an hour since she met the shuttle in Bay Two, but she already felt more energized and optimistic than she had in the last month. It felt right to have the admiral back on board the cruiser, and she knew the rest of the crew would be feeling the same way.

FOUR

Tuya Sansar was still fuming. She'd spent weeks talking to the voice through the grate, convinced she had finally connected with the brother that she hadn't seen in eight years. Hadn't been in the same room with in twelve. Instead, it turned out to be the traitor who'd sold out both crews and was responsible for Altan being imprisoned in the first place. Mad as a hatter, to boot. Her hands kept clenching, and she wished she could have gotten close enough to wrap them around the scrawny traitor's neck.

She had managed to hear her brother's voice, though. It was the one happy moment to come out of the entire debacle, hearing Altan before the guards pushed them back into their cells. She thought the Marine pointing a stun pistol into the room she'd heard the voice come from had fired, but she wasn't sure since she was struggling against a couple of soldiers at the time. They'd shoved her back into the cell, tossed her on the bed, and spit out a string of curses promising harsh punishment if she tried to escape again.

The cell felt even smaller now, as she paced back and forth. She managed to get six steps before having to turn and walk back to the other side. Six steps she'd made at least a few thousand times in the days since hearing Altan's voice. After pushing herself to build up strength following the removal of her cybernetic implants, she felt restless in her cage. Like a lion forced to look through the bars at all the appetizing snacks walking by.

There had to be some other way to get out of the short corridor of cells. She thought back to her original plan, the one she'd concocted after infiltrating the crew as someone coming off the frigates that brought hundreds of new people to the cruiser during its journey from the asteroid belt. She'd been smuggling parts for a plasma torch into a storage closet nearby, planning to cut her way into the service tunnels and find her brother's cell. It had seemed like a good plan, but after several weeks of being cooped up in one she knew it was overly ambitious.

She thought about faking an illness. A trip to the nearest medical bay would give her a slight chance of escaping, and if they brought a doctor or nurse into her cell it would give her a hostage to use as leverage to try something. But she was afraid the Marine guards wouldn't care enough to attempt getting her treatment. She'd noticed their attitudes growing more lax and unfeeling since the ship reached Earth.

Tuya growled in frustration, banging her fist against a metal bulkhead. There was little power behind it, her muscles still in the early stages of recovery from her surgery. In fact, she was starting to feel exhausted just from the pacing. Her thighs were quivering, and her calves felt like they were on fire.

She was just about to sit on the bunk to give her body a rest when she heard the clattering of the door's four magnetic locks being individually released. Tuya straightened, facing the door and tensing for what might be coming. The guards hadn't seemed overly upset since the escape attempt, but she knew how soldiers could hold grudges. Or perhaps Richard was being tortured somewhere and telling them it had all been her idea.

When the cell door slid open, two Marines were standing just outside. One was holding a stun pistol loosely, pointed at the floor but ready to raise and fire in half a second. The other was holding a pair of restraints. "Approach, prisoner."

Tuya eyed the restraints, considering whether she should rush the Marines and try to barge through them into the corridor. But she knew there would be at least one other soldier standing guard at the end of the corridor. She grit her teeth and complied with the order, walking slowly forward and holding her wrists in front of her stomach. The restraints were cold on her skin, the edges of the plastic rough as they rubbed against her hands and wrists. Once they were tightened and locked, the Marine grabbed her arm and pulled her into the corridor.

A third Marine was waiting just outside the door, this one also holding a stun pistol. Tuya was surprised to see them treating her with such caution, but also angry at the thought of where they might be taking her. She'd endured torture on the *Indomitable* once before, and wasn't looking forward to repeating the experience without the pain dampening effects of her implants. She glared at each of the Marines defiantly, then looked around the hallway.

The console at the rear where a Marine usually sat to monitor and control access to the cells was vacant. There were a couple more Marines at the opposite end, though, where the short security hall met the main corridor. A disheveled man was standing next to one soldier, complaining about something as he twisted his wrists in restraints. Not far from him was a zoned out woman who had the look of a drug fiend. She kept asking the prisoner next to her if he was carrying a hit of zoom. The final Marine was on the other side of that man, his gaze directed further down the corridor.

Tuya's glare stopped, and she felt her eyes go wide as she looked back at the man standing near the drug addict. He was average height, with dark hair that had grown long during his confinement. His face was turned toward her, a secret smile on lips beneath features that were so like her own. "Altan," she whispered.

He nodded, raising his bound hands to rub at his nose and gesture for her to stay quiet. She was so amazed to see him that she almost called out his name again, fighting a strong desire to run forward and throw her arms around him. The restraints digging into her skin brought her back to where she was, and she lowered her head in acknowledgement. The Marine holding her arm pushed her toward the small group of prisoners, and Tuya managed to adjust the course enough to end up beside Altan. She couldn't drag her eyes away from his face.

"Alright," one of the marines said. She seemed to be in charge of the other four. "We're going to lead these prisoners to the location specified in the transfer orders." Turning, she spoke directly to them. "If any of you give us the slightest bit of trouble, you're going to arrive with a bloody lip. More, if you continue to be difficult. Is that understood?"

The Marine didn't wait for an answer, waving as she took a left into the wide corridor. The other soldiers followed, two beside the prisoners and two behind with stun pistols unholstered. Tuya could hear the disheveled man complaining to someone called Mika that he was supposed to be released soon, but she tuned it out as she kept glancing over at Altan. Their arms rubbed together as they walked, and she reveled in the contact.

She had thought him dead for so long, after the remains of the ship he was on had been found. The *Telemachus* had been presumed destroyed when it collided with an errant asteroid, though no one could ever say for certain. The few remnants of the ship that were found couldn't point to any specific cause. Her desire to join him in the trade lanes turned into anger, and a determination to honor his memory in the only way she knew how. By joining a Guild ship.

The walk through the corridors was long, but Tuya was unable to focus on anything around them. If the Marines had suddenly scattered and run away, she never would have been able to tell where she was on the massive cruiser. But she didn't care, because she'd be with Altan at last. She kept fantasizing about calling their parents with the news that their son was still alive. That thought brought up the startling idea that after so long without hearing from her, they might be wondering if both their children were now dead.

"Halt!" the corporal in charge of the half-strength squad barked. There was a full squad of Marines approaching from the opposite direction, guiding a grossly obese man toward the entrance of a cargo bay. The man was struggling against the grip of the soldiers, screaming obscenities and threats as they disappeared through the portal.

The group of prisoners was led through the same doors a minute later, and Tuya took her eyes away from Altan long enough to glance at the vast openness. The deck was larger than any other cargo bay she'd ever been in, with only a single battered cargo shuttle occupying it. The ramp was extended, and two Marines were pushing the heavyset man up it. He was protesting the entire way, using his bulk to push the Marines off balance as he bellowed at them to obey his commands. "I'll have you guarding a shit pile in the middle of the desert, you brainless morons. I'm your captain!"

Tuya was shocked to realize the man was Guildersen, the officer she'd first encountered when the *Vagabond* arrived with a cargo pod destined for the Syndicate cruiser. She'd heard many things about him in her short time as a member of the crew, none of them good. She wondered how such a man could have been promoted to captain; she'd been baffled that he'd managed to rise to commander and XO of the most important ship in the system.

The Marine closest to her was snickering quietly, and she shared a confused look with her brother as they stood watching Guildersen disappear into the shuttle. "What's going on?" she asked under her breath.

"No idea," Altan whispered. "I just hope we're going to be on that shuttle when it leaves the ship."

She faintly hoped for the same outcome, but wondered where the shuttle might be heading if they were sticking a senior officer on it. The last thing they needed was to somehow escape the *Indomitable* just to end up in some high security detainment center in the middle of nowhere. When the corporal motioned for the group to follow her up the ramp, Tuya could only say a silent prayer and hope for the best.

The interior of the shuttle was in even worse condition than the outside. The decking was bare metal, covered in dents and scrapes from all the cargo hauled during the years.

The walls were rougher, with the inner hull gouged open in some spots. One hole was wide enough that she could even see the outer hull on the other side of the inch wide gap that separated the two skins of the ship.

The shuttle pilot was staring at the still struggling Guildersen in confusion as the four other prisoners were escorted up the ramp, turning with raised eyebrows as they entered the shuttle. "Uh, what's going on, fellas? This ain't exactly a luxury transport."

"Prisoner transfer," the corporal said, her tone making it clear she was eager to get this over with and move on to more exciting jobs. "Four going Earth-side."

The shuttle pilot looked around and shrugged. "Let me get some jump seats set up for you. I wasn't expecting more company after this one." He hooked a thumb at Guildersen, sitting next to an unconscious man in an expensive business suit.

While the seats were being prepared, the corporal stepped over to stand a few feet away from the fat man. He stopped his struggles and yelling to look up at her visor, a wide sneer on his face. "Guildersen," the woman said. "I guess you can't bully your way out of this one. You fat, disgusting pig."

The man's face grew redder with each word, his chins wobbling as he seethed. "I want your name, corporal. You just earned a dishonorable discharge and time in the worst prison I can find."

"Corporal Diana Velez," the Marine said with a smirk visible just below her face shield. "Good luck finding me. You fucking maggot." She hawked up a thick wad of phlegm and spat it at his face. Then she turned and walked away, impervious to the yells and obscenities thrown at her back.

The pilot made short work of extending a few extra seats, and the four prisoners were shoved into them. Tuya made sure she got the spot next to Altan, directly across from Guildersen. His shouts and shrieks stopped for a moment, and she saw recognition flare in his eyes as he looked at her. She gave a smirk, raising her restrained hands to give him both middle fingers. That set him off on another apoplectic fit of rage.

She didn't hear a word of it, enjoying the feel of her brother's shoulder rubbing against hers. Part of her was still trying to say this was nothing but a dream, as the Marines snapped restraints around each of their chests to hold them in the seats while the shuttle descended to the planet. The straps were tight against her chest and stomach, but she pushed against them enough to lean her head against Altan's.

"Altan," she said in a cracking voice. "I never thought I'd get to see you again, big brother."

"I thought the same thing for too long, little sister. You don't know how great it is to have you with me now."

"Well, the circumstances could be better," she said with a laugh. "We don't even know where this shuttle is taking us."

"Away from here," he said. "And we're going together. That's all that matters."

FIVE

Ensign Robert Graves sighed for at least the hundredth time since the start of his shift. He'd spent several years at the Academy studying reactor physics and engine mechanics, but it was done more as something to fill the time than because he had a real interest in it. Now he was in charge of the Engineering section aboard the frigate *Waterloo*, trying to dig forgotten knowledge out of his brain every day.

When the ship had been boarded by Syndicate soldiers, the Chief Engineer had been killed along with many Marines and more than a dozen people on the bridge. By the time the Coalition crew had regained control, the most senior officer in Engineering was also the woman promoted to XO of the ship. Graves had been selected as temporary head of the section, with the expectation that as soon as they returned to Earth a replacement could be quickly shipped up.

Instead, the *Waterloo* was now pledging loyalty to the splinter government on Luna, led by former Defense Minister Rinde Brighton. There would be no shipment of new recruits, no replacement for the job that had become his permanent home.

To be fair, Graves didn't mind working in Engineering too much. Most of the problems he encountered on a normal day were interesting, and they stimulated his curiosity as he worked to figure out solutions to them. He even enjoyed learning about the new deuterium-powered fusion reactor that had been installed in the frigate to get them quickly back to Earth. The amount of energy created was exciting, especially when he let his imagination run free with all the possibilities that could be made into reality because of it.

His major problem lately was the man who had come along with the reactor, Dr. Wilhelm Francks. The physicist from Berlin was highly protective of the reactor he'd helped to finish the research on and build. The Silva Reactor was the brainchild of a researcher named Robert Silva, killed on Interamnia when the *Indomitable* destroyed the asteroid colony. His incomplete research was sent to the Guild before his death, and they reached out to trusted contacts to complete the work.

"No, no, no," Dr. Francks cried, waving his arms as he hurried across the engine room. Graves sighed as he left his console to follow behind and try to smooth over whatever had irritated the physicist now. "You must not adjust the power flow from the reactor in such a way. This will require more testing, careful modification, and a guiding hand. Yes?"

The crewwoman the physicist was berating looked back with tired eyes. After a week of suffering through his motherly ministrations, everyone in Engineering had become inured to Dr. Francks' frequent outbursts. Graves inserted himself between the two when the wild-haired physicist looked ready to start another lecture about how to properly handle new technology. "Dr. Francks, can we speak? Over at my station."

Graves led the older man back to the row of terminals, out of the flow of crew working to complete their daily tasks to maintain the engines. The physicist kept his gaze on the reactor housing, glaring at the crewwoman who had turned back to the display and continued typing in the commands to complete whatever job she'd been assigned.

"All these changes should go through me," Dr. Francks protested. "Why do you let these untrained children touch something so delicate and precise?"

"Doctor, these men and women have gone through the Academy and been trained in engine and reactor mechanics. They may not have the knowledge to build a reactor, but they know how to keep it running smoothly with the ship's systems." Graves got the physicist seated, and crossed his arms. "I know it's hard to turn over control, but it has to be done. If we ran every request through you, there'd never be any time for you to eat or sleep."

"Sleep? You think I sleep when I have nightmares about grubby fingers telling my reactor to do things it cannot do? You must lock down that panel, and let me decide what new commands we send into the reactor software."

"No, sir," Graves said, reaching up to pinch the bridge of his nose with frustration. "Must I remind you that you're on the *Waterloo* in a purely observational capacity? The contract we signed with the Guild, or I guess the Colonial Alliance now, stipulated that we have control over how the reactor is used."

Dr. Francks looked indignant at those words, and his face turned a vivid shade of scarlet. "If you will not listen to expert advice, ensign, then I would rather not be here at all."

I'd happily stick you in a shuttle myself, Graves thought, fantasizing about waving as it disappeared through the ion barrier in the docking bay. "I am more than happy to listen to your advice, sir, as long as you realize that I can't always take it. This is a frigate, built for patrol and protection, not a test ship that can afford to lose power for hours at a time while you test every new change."

Sighing again, he sat at the next station. "How about we discuss all the proposed improvements my people have been coming up with? Have you had time to look through the ideas for increasing the power flow to the railguns?"

The physicist's eyes lit up, and Graves was glad to see he'd managed to deflect the man's attention. Even if it would only last until he solved whichever idea he latched onto. Hopefully it would be one that took him days instead of hours. If he figured out one of the big ones, it could go a long way to helping them in the war.

"There was something interesting one of your people mentioned in the galley a few nights ago," Dr. Francks said musingly. "He assumed it was possible to increase power to the railguns in such a way as to triple the speed with which they can eject a round, which it theoretically is. Then he asked if we could use that same power to launch more than one projectile at once. I admit it was an intriguing idea. We've always known that an increased projectile weight requires an exponential increase in energy to push it through the tube. But if we could configure the reactor to..."

Graves knew the physicist would be lost in his own little world for a while, and took the opportunity to switch his work over to the station he was sitting at. He had pages of reports to look through, with requests for supplies that were running low in the ship's onboard stocks. It had been more than a month since they last got a supply shipment from Earth, and the way things were looking it could be months more before they could count on another. He had to figure out how to get all the necessary work done maintaining the ship's engines and systems while still shepherding the resources available.

He was interrupted half an hour later when one of the crew working on the roving repair teams touched his shoulder. "Rafferty. What's going on?"

"Sorry to bug you, ensign, but I wanted to see if anyone has let you know we used up the last of the fiber cable rolls today."

"What?" Graves turned back to his station and scrolled through the work orders. He found one marked as completed, with a small note about using up the last cabling. Groaning, he rubbed a hand over his face. "Thanks for letting me know, Rafferty. I'll see what I can do about getting some more."

As he scrolled through the latest completed work orders, he saw several more notes about supplies that were very low or now expended. Releasing yet another sigh, Graves resigned himself to having to place a call to the bridge. He'd need to ask the XO about getting what was needed to keep the ship functional. The only saving grace was that Commander Richtaus had served in Engineering for years and knew how vital these things could be.

He could only hope the Alliance was able to work with them to get the supplies they needed. Otherwise, the *Waterloo* was one bad break away from being useless when the inevitable fight against the *Indomitable* started.

Six

Vegley took a deep breath and enjoyed the serenity she felt standing by the rail of the command deck. Not having to worry about Guildersen storming through the door raging about some petty thing or other was letting her actually enjoy the job of being executive officer on the largest ship in the system. For the first time, she felt as if she truly belonged in her exalted position.

She heard the hiss of a door opening, and turned to see Admiral Yumata exiting from the office attached to his quarters. "Commander," he said in greeting as he stopped beside her. His hands were clasped behind his back, and he almost looked to be preening. Vegley knew how he must be feeling, returned to the ship he'd been instrumental in creating.

"Admiral. Have you heard from the committees yet?"

"Selene has been trying to contact me," he said, referring to the head of the Military Committee. "They expected this trip to last no more than a few hours, and are now demanding to know why the shuttle hasn't left for the return trip to Earth yet. She also wants to know why Abernathy isn't answering his calls."

"Should we oblige them and release the shuttle? I can instruct the pilot to drop his unwanted passengers somewhere out of the way. That should give us more time before the leadership realizes there's been a mutiny aboard the *Indomitable*." Vegley relished the thought of Guildersen being dropped off in the middle of the wilderness somewhere, no idea where he was or how to get back to civilization. She wondered how long he might last in such a situation. *Probably longer than he'd wish. After all, he has all that fat to sustain him for days and days.*

"Soon, commander." Yumata turned to glance at her. "What are your thoughts on this proclamation from Luna? The Coalition splinter government, and formation of the new Colonial Alliance?"

She pursed her lips in thought. Everyone on the cruiser had seen the announcement, or caught replays of it. She had personally watched it several times, examining every detail, looking to see if the man Brighton were sincere or just serving as a mouthpiece for the Transport Guild. She refused to accept their usurpation of control over the asteroid mining colonies, Luna, and Mars. "Sir, I believe it's no more than propaganda. Political theater as one faction of their government tries to wrest power from another. As for this Alliance nonsense..." She snorted, shaking her head in disgust. "I would call it an obvious attempt to sow more chaos in a situation already out their control."

Yumata made a sound of disagreement. "I believe they are in earnest, commander."

"How?" she asked. "They may claim control over all settlements off Earth, but there's no way to enforce that. A ragtag group of freighters could never stand against the *Indomitable*, no matter how many peashooter railguns they install. An hour under our weapons, and they would run to the darkest corners they could find."

"You forget that we are currently without a home ourselves," Yumata said with a tight smile. "We have gone against the will of the Executive Committee, and there is no turning back. At this moment, we are a ship without a governmental will to enforce."

Vegley opened her mouth to reply, then closed it. She had never really considered the final consequences of her actions. Sure, they would be locked in restraints and taken to the brig if the mutiny failed. Beyond that, though, there would be lengthy trials. Yumata and the senior officers would be paraded before the Syndicate people as examples. More than likely, evidence would be "discovered" that showed they were in the employ of Coalition masters. It would be just one more way to show the depravity of their enemies. One more way to make the people want to fight.

"Yes, you see now where we stand. The Executive Committee will not be able to sit idly by and watch their last ship fall into the hands of mutineers. If the Coalition government discovered the situation, it is entirely possible their prime minister would see his bargain as a losing proposition. Then he would release the brakes he has been putting on the military reaction to our invasion."

"They have no choice, sir. The Syndicate has no other ships to send against us."

"Hmm, we shall see." Yumata didn't look convinced. She'd never worked closely with the admiral, having joined the ship with the Syndicate frigates that carried extra personnel out during the cruiser's trip to Earth. Even then, she had worked at one of the stations at the rear of the command deck and saw him from that perspective. Her promotion to XO had been solely due to being the only officer at the rank of commander on the ship when Guildersen became the captain. The last few hours had taught her to respect the admiral's keen mind.

"We do still have half a squadron of Darts, admiral. I could have a few of them patrolling around the ship at all times to ensure we aren't surprised by any attempts to seize control."

Yumata jerked his chin down once. "That is an excellent idea, commander."

Vegley stood beside him in silence for several seconds. "So, what *should* we do with the shuttle?"

The admiral turned on his heel, walking back toward his office. "I have an idea of where to send it. Tell the pilot he will have his orders in twenty minutes." As he disappeared into his private chambers, Vegley stared at the door. She was trying to guess at his thoughts, but could come up with nothing. She just hoped they wouldn't send her former commander to a comfortable destination. If she didn't fear it would make her just as bad as him, she'd push to toss him out of the airlock as Guildersen had done to so many others.

She strode to the row of consoles, bending over the lieutenant occupying the communications station to relay the admiral's words to the shuttle pilot.

Half an hour later, she watched as the shuttle departed. Displays filled every inch of wall space along the sides and front of the bridge, giving the feel that the viewer was merely looking through transparent materials at everything outside the cruiser. It was one of the things she loved most about standing at the command deck rail, gazing out at the majestic field of stars when the ship was facing toward the outer system. At other times, the displays had to be darkened as the sun passed through them.

"Excellent, I see our guests have made their exit."

Vegley turned to look at the admiral, surprised by his sudden appearance. "Yes, sir. I notice the shuttle is not on course for a direct landing." She made it a statement, but knew he had to hear the question in her words.

"No, commander. They will be landing quite far from where they are expected." Yumata's lips were upturned slightly, as close as he came to showing amusement. "Any status updates on repairs to our weapons systems?"

"Work crews have been dispatched to emplacements three and eight. The railgun components are being transferred, and should be in place to begin installation within the hour. ETA for completion of the work is seventeen hours."

"Excellent job, Commander Vegley." He turned to raise an eyebrow at her. "We never had a chance to become acquainted before I was removed from command, but I think Guildersen made at least one good decision in promoting you to XO."

She laughed bitterly. "He had no say in it, sir. I was the next in line by order of seniority, and his orders were to use the personnel on board."

"Then I must be grateful for that order. You have proven yourself to be a wonderful XO, so far. I believe we will work very well together. The *Indomitable* will be well served with the two of us in command."

"Thank you, sir." Vegley felt herself standing straighter with pride. She knew that whatever plans the admiral came up with for the cruiser, she'd be behind them. Yumata was the epitome of the efficient officer she'd always imagined serving under, the kind of man who thought about his crew and his ship with equal affection.

SEVEN

Erik stepped through the doors of the Aldrin administration building, craning his head to look at the detailed mural painted on one wall. It showed the evolution of Luna, from the first lander on the moon to the two domes side by side. He wanted to spend more time looking at each panel, but a tug on his hand reminded him that it would have to wait for another day.

After the fourth descent to Earth to scoop up rescued factory workers, he departed the ship to help out in the dome. Mira was in charge of the *Vagabond* for the next couple of trips.

"It looks like they left the place a mess," Dex said. She was staring at the scattered papers and broken electronics that covered the reception desk and floor.

"Yeah, they were definitely in a hurry to leave." Erik gestured at a door hanging from a single hinge. One of the panels on it was splintered, and looked as if someone had put a fist through it. They wandered around the building, with Dex making notes on her tablet about repairs that would be necessary before the building could be used.

After forming the Alliance, President Meyers had dispatched five ships to the mining colonies on Vesta, Hygeia, Cybele, Davida, and Ceres. They were still small settlements, with the largest barely surpassing five hundred people. The Coalition and Syndicate had given them few resources before the colonies broke free to govern themselves independently, and it had only gotten harder to attract new citizens after that. Meyers had plans to change that, and the first step was getting a representative from each colony to Luna so they could all meet and ratify a charter of laws for the new government.

Meyers wanted the former Coalition administration center cleared out and prepared by the time those representatives arrived. They needed the extra space for the additional people the Alliance would have to bring in to help with running the government. He also wanted a set of offices for Rinde Brighton to run his competing Coalition government from in the short term.

"How long do you think it will be before Brighton can go to Earth?" Erik asked, gathering pages of loose paper while Dex made notes about the room they were in.

"It probably won't be soon," she said distractedly. "The leaders of some Coalition ground forces have finally united behind a general who is ignoring the order to remain in a protective formation around Geneva, but they're still outnumbered by the Syndicate forces. Three to one, according to our latest intel reports."

He snorted in amusement. "Sorry, it just sounds weird to talk about intel reports. This time last year I was just a simple transport captain carrying cargo to my next destination. Now we're talking about making new laws and creating a fleet. Never would have expected this much change in so short a time."

"No one would," Dex said, smiling over at him before turning back to her tablet. "It had to be done, though. People on Earth are too focused on themselves, and never think about those of us living beyond the atmosphere."

Erik nodded, even though he knew she wasn't looking in his direction. He read scattered lines across each page as he picked them up, optimistically hoping he'd come across something important. Most of the documents in this room were about supply shipments and updates on the count of items on hand. He was thinking this must have been a quartermaster's office of some sort.

Footsteps alerted him to a new arrival, and he looked up in time to see two armored soldiers pass by the door. The man following them stopped to lean against the doorframe. "She already has you taking out the trash, huh?"

"Her wish is my command," Erik said with a grin. He stood up and dropped the stack of papers on the desk before crossing the room to shake hands. "How are you doing, Tom?"

"Pretty good. I've got a fifth squad, now that we scraped together ten more recruits. Some of the new folks over in Armstrong have been asking about joining, as well. So I might get a couple more squads formed, if they do." Captain Tom Fitz nodded at Dex when she looked up from her tablet. "Ma'am. We've swept this floor for audio and video bugs, and we're moving upstairs. Nothing yet, so either the Coalition didn't leave any behind or knew how to hide them from our scanners."

"Thank you, Tom. Send in a report once you're done. President Meyers may want to dig deeper before we start using any of these offices, though."

He raised a fist to his chest and lowered it in a wave as he left to catch up with the militia soldiers running the scanning equipment. Erik couldn't stop a swell of pride at how well the man had taken to the role of militia leader. Although, he supposed it was no longer a militia now that they'd formed a real government. A fancy name for the

Alliance military would probably be devised during the meetings that also created the charter.

"What do you think of this office?" Dex asked, looking at the walls and the window that looked out on the central square.

"It's a nice one," Erik said. "I can imagine your desk right here, so you can look out on the square the few times you look up from your work. Lots of space for the secure server you have next to your desk in the Guildhall." He smiled, stepping closer to wrap an arm around her shoulders. "It's a good comfortable office for the vice president of the Alliance."

Dex laughed, a melodious sound that always sent shivers of pleasure up his spine. She poked him in the ribs, looking up at him with sparkling eyes. "Not for me, sweetie. For you."

"Me?" Erik looked at the office with a new perspective. He'd never thought about having his own space in the dome before. Before he started dating Dex, whenever his ship was docked on Luna he would always spend most of his day enjoying entertainment options and then head back to the *Vagabond* to sleep in his cabin. These days he spent his nights in Dex's apartment, but also went back onboard the freighter when he had work that needed to be done there. "Why would I need an office?"

"You're in command of the fleet," she said gently. "It may not be much yet, but it'll grow. When it does, you're going to have a lot of extra responsibility on your plate. It'll be much easier to run things from Luna than trying to coordinate it all from the *Vagabond*."

He felt a stab of pain in his stomach at the thought of leaving his ship. He'd lived and worked in space since his father purchased an old freighter and took him off Earth when he was eleven. He could barely remember his life before that now, and the longest he'd ever been away from a ship was the days spent imprisoned aboard the *Indomitable* when they discovered it in the asteroid belt. Could he really handle a job that kept him chained to a desk?

"You won't have to be here constantly," Dex said quietly, as if reading her mind. "But there will be times when we need you on Luna to coordinate fleet movements, or when we start building patrol ships. Not that I wouldn't be glad to see more of you."

"I'd love to see more of you, too," he told her, squeezing her against him. "This is just a big change. I don't even know if I'm that good of a captain with one ship, much less trying to give orders to a fleet."

"Erik, you are a great captain. Every person on the *Vagabond* would tell you that. You don't let the power go to your head, and that's what makes you one of the good ones." She reached up to tap his temple, and then went up on her toes to give him a quick kiss. "Okay, let's head upstairs and see what that looks like. A few more hours and we should be done."

Her estimate turned out to be overly optimistic, which he knew as soon as they got to the top of the stairs and found Tom waiting with a hand out. He shook his head. "We found the bugs. Main conference room up here is covered with them, as is the big corner office."

"The one they'd expect Meyers to take," Erik said. It made sense. The Coalition administrator had to realize what direction things were moving when she fled the dome, and anticipated the day the Guild finally moved in to take over the building.

Dex was looking in the direction of that office, her eyes unfocused as she thought through the ramifications. "Okay, let's get a demolition team in here, Captain Fitz. Tear down the walls in every room on this level, make sure there aren't any devices hidden where the scanners wouldn't find them. If we find more than a handful, do the same to the first floor."

"Yes, ma'am. It's going to take a few days, and will set back the repairs and reopening."

"That won't be a problem. President Meyers and I added in a cushion for any unexpected issues we came across, and both of us thought this kind of thing most likely. Let me know when the full sweep is complete, and I'll finish my inventory of the building then."

Tom saluted, turning away to pass the new orders to the soldiers running the scans. Erik was smirking at Dex when she turned to look at him, and she raised her eyebrows. "What?"

"Nothing," he said, raising his hands. "You're just incredibly sexy when you're giving orders, that's all."

"Oh yeah?" She reached out to poke him in the chest. "I'll remember that when we get home tonight, mister. See how you like me giving orders then."

"I think I'll like it a lot," he said around a laugh. As he followed her back down the stairs and through the main doors of the building, Erik couldn't help but think there were a few perks to a job that might keep him dirtside more often than he'd like. The kind of perks he could get accustomed to pretty easily.

As soon as they entered the Alliance Hall, someone rushed over to meet them. "Ms. Avila, the XO of the *Waterloo* has been trying to get in contact. She'd like you to call as soon as you can."

Dex acknowledged the request, leading Erik into the office she shared with Meyers. The Alliance president was out visiting the newest residents of Armstrong dome with Prime Minister Brighton, the latest rescues from the factory the Coalition leadership had been using to punish political rivals and dissidents. With the door closed, she approached the large screen on the main wall and keyed in the commands to call the frigate in orbit around Luna.

Moments later, Commander Mags Richtaus filled the screen. She was scowling, but Erik couldn't decide if it was frustration with them for taking so long to reply or about the issue she was reporting. "Madam Vice President, Captain Frost. Twenty three minutes ago, our sensors picked up a shuttle departing the *Indomitable*. We were unable to get a visual since it exited on the far side of the cruiser, but we're fairly certain it was the cargo shuttle that arrived early this morning."

"Why is this interesting news, commander?" Dex's brows were furrowed, and Erik could see she was trying to come up with a reason for the report.

Mags stared at the screen for several seconds, biting her lip as she came to a decision. "Ma'am, I'm going to tell you this in the strictest confidence. It's something that no one outside of Admiral Holgerson, Captain Andrews, myself, and our senior intelligence officer knows."

Dex nodded solemnly. "Whatever you tell us will go no farther than this room, commander. You have my word."

"We have been receiving data bursts from the *Indomitable*. It started almost as soon as we arrived, and at first we thought it must be an attempt at misinformation. Each burst is a short report, much like the fleet intelligence division used to send out. We've been able to verify some of the data received, and feel that it is accurate. For instance, yesterday's report told us about three railguns that were nonfunctional and only made to look operational. A closer scan of those emplacements verified the weapons are damaged in such a way as to present no danger."

"That's a great source," Erik said, shocked at the turn of events. "Do you have any idea who could be sending this data?"

"No, Captain Frost. Admiral Holgerson thinks it might be an operative planted by Intelligence at some point, perhaps when the Syndicate frigates transported personnel to the cruiser. Whoever it is must not realize that the *Waterloo* is working with the splinter government, or they agree with our views on the matter. Whatever the case, we're happy to have the information."

Mags paused, examining both of them on the screen before continuing. "We received a data burst forty five minutes ago. The data included tells us that Admiral Yumata has returned to the *Indomitable*. Not only that, he led a mutiny against the captain, who was his former first officer. The intel in the burst also says that Captain Guildersen was placed on the cargo shuttle along with a Military Committee member who traveled with Yumata." She paused again, locking her gaze on Erik. "There were four other prisoners placed on the shuttle. Two of them I've never heard of, but the other two I think you know."

He gasped, knowing there were only two names that he could care about from that ship. "Tuya."

"Yes, Captain Frost. Altan and Tuya Sansar are on that shuttle, heading for Earth."

EIGHT

Tuya felt the shuttle vibrate as it lifted from the deck. She knew she should be worried about where it might be taking them, but she was too happy to be with her brother again to care. They could be dropped off right in the Executive Committee chambers, and she would still be smiling. As the shuttle passed through the ion barrier, shuddering a bit with the transition, she only leaned her head over as far as she could to touch his.

The man and woman who had shared the cell block with them were yelling, confusion and anger in their voices. They kept demanding to know where they were going, and the woman would pepper her demands with requests for drugs. Her voice had gone wavery, and Tuya could see sweat pouring down the woman's face when she glanced over. Withdrawal symptoms, for sure.

"Whass goong on?" The voice came from the man in a business suit, and she saw his eyes blink open before squeezing closed again. After half a minute, he tried again. Blinking rapidly, the man turned his head slowly to get a look at who else was in the shuttle. When he saw the fat man beside him, his eyes locked in. "Captain Guildersen? Where are we?"

"The same shuttle you brought Yumata to my ship on," Guildersen said through gritted teeth. "You were supposed to keep him on a tight leash, Abernathy. Not let him lead a mutiny."

"He promised it was just a short trip to talk the officers into cooperating with you." Abernathy's voice had a whining quality that was grating to Tuya's ears. She could imagine him growing up as the spoiled scion of some obscenely wealthy family. The kind of man who was accustomed to everyone doing what he told them to do. "Mrs. Onassis is not going to be happy about this."

"No, the chairwoman will most decidedly not be happy. You're going to be lucky if they only kick you off the committee." Guildersen's face was growing redder with every word. Tuya wondered if she might get to watch him have a stroke. She thought she might enjoy that.

"She can't kick me off the committee. My dad paid handsomely for that seat." Abernathy looked away from the fat man at last, looking at the four people strapped in across from him. "Who are these people?" She could hear the sneer in his voice, the disdain of sharing a shuttle with people who were obviously far below his social station.

"Don't worry about them!" Guildersen yelled. "They're scum. Traitors and addicts. Nothing. Worry about how we're going to get the *Indomitable* back!"

"You and I can convince the Executive committee to authorize a strike team," Abernathy said dismissively. "We'll take a dozen shuttles, two dozen squads of soldiers, and be back in control by this time tomorrow."

"Are you really that stupid?" Guildersen's voice had gone quiet, and Tuya couldn't help but think that was a dangerous thing in a man with a volatile temper. "The railguns may be damaged, but most of the defensive weaponry is still operational. We'd be lucky to get half those shuttles close to the cruiser."

"So we send more," Abernathy said, his voice going high pitched with panic. Tuya could see it in his eyes now, the way his pupils were expanding and contracting rapidly as he stared around at them. "We send every shuttle we have. They can't shoot them all down."

"No, we just shoot *it* down instead. Kill all of the mutinous traitors." Guildersen was snarling now, and seemed to look right at her with the last words.

Abernathy and Guildersen continued to talk, but their words were drowned out as the shuttle passed through Earth's atmosphere. The turbulence was enough to jar her head as it bounced against Altan's, and she reluctantly pulled away. Cargo shuttles such as this were built with heat shields to absorb or deflect most of the high temperatures generated by atmospheric entry, but as she felt the interior begin to warm she thought it might be time to consider replacing them.

The shuttle jerked beneath them a few times, pushing her against the straps over her chest and stomach. Tuya kept her jaw clenched to keep her teeth from rattling, smiling as she saw a trickle of blood from Abernathy's mouth. The fool kept talking, and bit his tongue a second time when the braking thrusters fired. She heard him cursing, and got the impression that sort of thing happened to him a lot.

As the shuttle slowed, the turbulence also lessened. She could hear air flowing over the surface of the ship, and wished there were windows in the compartment to allow her to see where they might be going. She tuned out the four different voices with their various complaints and demands, leaning against Altan again.

It seemed only seconds later when she felt a gentle bump, and the hum of the thrusters faded away to be replaced by a ticking sound as the hull plates continued to cool from reentry. There was a faint ozone odor, but it was overridden by years of grease and other smells from the multitude of cargo containers the shuttle had carried.

"Alright, folks. We've reached your final destination." The pilot spoke with a chipper tone, but Tuya could see wariness in his eyes. He kept a hand close to the stun pistol strapped around his waist, as well. He punched a few keys on a small pad, and the shuttle's door slowly lowered. The interior was flooded with late afternoon sunlight and the smell of grass. Real grass, not the hydroponic imitation that some people would grow on Luna and the colonies.

The pilot looked over his six passengers with squinted eyes. "I'm going to release you, and you're going to walk down that ramp. The controls are locked, so you couldn't go anywhere if you did try to overpower me. Once I'm back in the air, my orders are to wait thirty minutes and then call in your position to the local authorities." He glanced at each of them for a few seconds, as if looking for evidence that his words had sunk in. "Walk down the ramp and be picked up in an hour, or fight me and have to walk back to civilization."

With his words echoing in the shuttle, the pilot tapped a button on the wall display. There was a loud click, and Tuya felt the restraints around her torso release. She hadn't realized until that moment how tight they had been, and she took in a deep breath of the fresh Earth air. Guildersen was the first on his feet, maneuvering his bulk toward the pilot with angry steps.

"You will return us to the *Indomitable* right now, or I will have your head. Do you hear me?"

The pilot barely flinched, smoothly drawing the stun pistol and raising it. "Keep moving, sir, or I'll have to make the others drag your unconscious body out."

Guildersen's face went red again, and he sputtered for a few seconds before he could get his words out. "I am a captain in the Syndicate fleet. You will obey my orders!"

"I don't work for the fleet," the pilot said calmly. "Last chance. Walk or drag, but either way you're exiting this shuttle."

Abernathy pushed past the large naval officer, jutting his face forward and stabbing a finger into the pilot's chest. "I am a member of the Military Committee. Do you understand what that means? If you don't take us to Hong Kong right now, you'll be convicted of kidnapping a committee member. Instant death, my friend."

The pilot laughed in his face. "Do you think I'll ever go back to Syndicate territory again after this? I don't know how I let Admiral Yumata talk me into this at all, but I know the kind of hell I'm in for if anyone ever finds out. Once I'm off the ground, you'll never see me again. Now move it, down the ramp."

Tuya glanced at Altan and shrugged. They rose from their seats just as the drug addict pushed past. "Get me off this thing," the woman screamed. "I feel them crawling on me. They're under my skin." There were trails of bloody scratch marks on her wrists, as far up as her restrained hands could reach. Her eyes were wild, and she didn't even stop as she bounced off Guildersen and ran down the ramp.

"Mika wouldn't do this to me," the last prisoner was moaning. "I'm supposed to be back on duty. Why would they send me off the ship?"

Altan was staring at him with desperate sadness, and Tuya realized it was the same look he'd always had as a kid when she got in trouble for something he did. "You did this," she said. "You got us transferred off the ship."

He grimaced and nodded. "I had to insert some code in the operating system to fake a transfer. I didn't know our cell numbers, so specified the entire corridor thinking it would just be you and me. These other two got scooped up last night, I guess. I didn't even know where they'd send us, I just wanted a transfer as far from the *Indomitable* as I could get."

She snorted and looked at the vast expanse of tall grass that was visible through the open hatch. "It looks like you got that wish. Don't feel bad, big brother. You did a good thing. I was starting to think I would never see you again, in spite of all the effort I put into trying to rescue you." It was her turn to grimace, and she felt a sourness in her mouth. "I was so close, until the wrong person saw me."

Altan reached out with his bound hands, grasping hers. "But we're together now. And not being delivered to a prison, by some miracle." He led her forward, past the still arguing Guildersen and Abernathy. They stood at the exit of the shuttle, blinking in the bright sunlight and taking in the uninterrupted expanse of grass and low hills that spread before them to the horizon. Low shrubs and stilted trees dotted the landscape.

Tuya gasped, looking at it all. "Altan, it looks like home."

"It does," he whispered reverently. "I never thought I'd see home again."

They walked slowly down the ramp, and Tuya paused at the bottom. When she finally reached out with a foot to touch the ground, she was afraid it would turn out to be a cruel dream. The kind of nightmare where you are so close to touching the thing you most want, and then wake up half a second before it happens. When her foot planted solidly on the ground, she felt nervous laughter bubbling out.

Altan fell to his knees beside her, reaching out to run his hands through the knee high stalks of grass. She followed his lead, plucking a strand of grass to hold it to her nose. It smelled so familiar, and yet not exactly the same. She wasn't sure if that was an indication of distance from the area they'd grown up, or because she'd been off Earth for more than seven years. Already, she could feel the strain of being under full gravity after years of quarter G thrusts.

There was a sizzling sound behind them, and Tuya jerked her head around to see Abernathy sliding down the ramp. His face was rubbing against the grated surface that gave better traction, and she knew he'd be bruised by tomorrow. Guildersen was backing out of the shuttle, still yelling at the pilot and threatening all kinds of punishments. Not too deep down, she was hoping the fat bastard would get a stun bolt himself. But he kept backing down the ramp until he was standing beside them.

The pilot disappeared from sight, and then reappeared pushing the last prisoner before him. The man was still moaning about Mika, and Tuya really wanted to slap him to shut him up by the time he was standing on the grass. The pilot stood just inside the hatch, his stun pistol back in the holster. "I'm just following my orders," he said, reaching up to press the button that started to close the ramp with the grinding noise of gears that needed to be greased.

"What about these?" Tuya yelled, holding up her hands to display the restraints. The pilot only shrugged before he disappeared from view. Altan grabbed her wrist, pulling her away. She stumbled along behind him, quickly getting out of the blast zone of the shuttle's thrusters. Guildersen remained standing where he'd stepped off the ramp, shaking a fist and yelling curses. Abernathy was crumpled near his feet.

There was a single high-pitched noise, and then the shuttle's thrusters fired and pushed it into the air. The pilot was being cautious, using a minimum amount of power, and that was the only thing that saved the officer. Guildersen was thrown onto his back, but was otherwise unscathed as the shuttle flew into north. Tuya snickered, then turned her back on the two entitled elites and walked with her brother.

"What season is it?" Altan asked. She could only shake her head, as clueless as he was. The one thing you never had to worry about in space was changing seasons. She couldn't even be sure of the date on the system standard calendar after being locked away so long. "It feels like fall, maybe late summer," her brother said, closing his eyes to feel the breeze on his face.

"Does it matter? We need to find out where we are. We can't wait for local authorities, Altan. If they run our names in the system, we'll be back in cells by nightfall."

He nodded, and leaned forward to push himself back to his feet. "You're right. I just wish I had some idea of where we are, which way to go. If we're in Mongolia, then we can't be too far from Ulaanbaatar. Only the northern part of the country looks like this."

"But we could be anywhere within a thousand kilometers north of the city," she said, finishing his thought. Tuya was scanning the horizon, wondering how much time they had left before the pilot alerted the authorities. Would he even do such a thing? She couldn't imagine the admiral having them dropped off in such a remote area if he really intended to tell people where they were. Looking over at Guildersen, she could well imagine wanting him to just disappear forever. It wasn't a chance they could afford to take, though.

"Over there," Altan said, raising his hands to point toward the tallest hill they could see. It looked to be a kilometer away, an easy walk even as their bodies were starting to feel the drag of gravity. He looked around at the others. The woman going through withdrawal was still scratching at her wrists as she rocked back and forth and mumbled to herself. The man from the cells was still complaining about Mika. Guildersen was groaning as he worked to push his bulk off the ground. Abernathy was still unconscious, the stun bolt sticking out of a bicep in a way that would generate a lot of pain when it was removed. "My sister and I are going to walk to that hill and try to get an idea of our location. Any of you are free to come with us, if you wish."

None of the others acted as if they'd even heard the words, except Guildersen who was sneering at them in disgust. Tuya smiled at him, a rictus grin that was almost a snarl. She turned away and started walking toward the distant hill without another word, and heard Altan follow a few seconds later.

While she walked, she examined the restraints around her wrists. The Marines hadn't used the powerful metal collars that would lock the entire forearm in place, instead choosing simple plastic ties that zipped tight. She thought she could work them loose if she kept at it long enough, but the rough edges were already starting to chafe her skin.

Altan jogged up to walk at her side, and she glanced over to see he had a stone in one hand. "It looks like flint," he explained. "If I can find a bigger rock to smash it against, we'll have some sharp edges to cut through these restraints."

They both kept on the lookout for such a rock, not seeing one until they were close to the hill. Altan tossed his stone at it four times before hitting it just right to split along an internal fault line. It broke into two halves, with tiny shards flying through the air. One of the shards slapped against Tuya's cheek, and she felt a tiny drop of blood welling up. She paid it no mind, though, stooping to pick up one half of the stone. There was a sharp edge perhaps an inch long, and she grasped the smooth stone in one hand to begin rubbing it against her plastic restraints as Altan did the same with the other half of the stone.

They continued walking, climbing the gentle slope of the hill. It took longer than she had expected, and by the time they reached the summit her wrist was bleeding but the plastic restraint was barely hanging on. Tuya held up a knee, and slammed her hands down on either side. Once, twice, a third time. The restraints snapped, and her hands were free. She yelled in triumph, turning to help Altan with his own.

Hands free, they embraced. Tuya leaned her head against her brother's chest, wrapping her arms tightly around him. "We're free," she whispered, over and over. "We're free."

Altan laughed, a joyous sound that lifted her own spirits. "Not only that, I think I know where we are now." She looked up at him in confusion, and he turned them so that she could look along his arm to a blue haze on the horizon. "I think that is Lake Baikal. Remember when we were kids, mom and dad dragged us there for a week each summer?"

Tuya snorted, smiling fondly at the memories. "I remember you telling me how it was the deepest lake in the world, and sea monsters lived in the depths waiting to swallow little girls who went swimming too far from the shore. I wouldn't even go near the water that summer."

He chuckled, pulling her close in a tight squeeze. "I'd forgotten that. But if I'm right, and that is Baikal, then we're only four or five hundred kilometers from home. We can walk there, sis."

She stared at the blue haze, hoping that Altan was right about what they were seeing. For the first time in too long, she thought about seeing her parents again. The tears her mother would cry to see her, the gruff way her father would greet her as if it was about time she visited. She wondered if even his stoic exterior would hold up when they saw the son they'd thought dead years before.

NINE

President Meyers leaned back in his chair, reaching up to rub his neck. He spent too many hours slumped over his tablet these days, and his muscles were protesting. He'd thought running the Transport Guild was a big job, juggling the ability to turn a profit for his captains while also keeping fees reasonable enough to generate more business. It was nothing compared to creating an Alliance to govern a planet, two moons, and five asteroids. Even if that planet was the most lightly populated of them all.

On top of it all, he was spending several hours each day with Rinde Brighton as they reached out to every contact the two of them had on Earth. He felt as if support for their splinter government was growing, but it wasn't fast enough. Every hour they spent trying to gain backing, the prime minister on the ground was growing more entrenched. The latest reports indicated he had moved his cabinet out of the capital, ostensibly because the Syndicate invasion force was now fighting against Coalition troops only a hundred kilometers away. He and Rinde both thought it was the prime minister's way of protecting himself against the Parliament that was growing increasingly weary of his new calls to surrender to the Syndicate.

That had been the man's reaction to the announcement that exposed his work camp factory, stuffed full of political rivals and anyone who spoke too loudly in opposition. The prime minister said it was a plot by an extremist faction within his own government, one intent on ripping the Coalition apart. His solution, the one that his conscience apparently demanded, was to surrender to the Syndicate so the two governments could join forces against such ignorance.

The most surprising thing had been the large number of people coming out in favor of the idea. The same people who were calling the Syndicate leaders corrupt corporate leeches a year ago now hailed them as saviors of the world's stability. News websites pivoted on a dime, churning out stories about separatist factions and the dangers of returning to the old world model. Meyers was baffled by it all, when nothing of the sort had even been intimated in Brighton's address.

He was working on a fifth draft of a new speech, one that he hoped to give alongside Brighton, a show of solidarity between the two new governments. Opinion was mixed on whether it would help or hinder the splinter government, with more people angry about the Alliance seemingly turning the rest of the system against the homeworld.

Dex burst into the office, with Captain Frost close behind. "Sir, the *Waterloo* just received another data burst from whatever operative is on the cruiser. They've confirmed that the ship's weapons were heavily damaged in the brief battles during it's trip to Earth. However, with the admiral back in charge the repairs are underway. Three railguns have been repaired or installed already, with two more in process."

"We have to move now," Frost said, leaning his hands on the glass topped desk. "If this information is correct, we have a chance against the *Indomitable* if we attack immediately. Any delay will just let them get more weapons operational."

Meyers groaned as he rubbed his neck harder. So much for working away the stress. What he'd just heard increased it threefold. "Did Commander Richtaus mention how Fleet Admiral Holgerson feels on the matter? Is he in favor of attack, as well? You know we can't do it without the *Waterloo*'s support."

Dex placed a hand on Frost's back, and he had the impression she was restraining him from launching into an impassioned plea. "Admiral Holgerson is hesitant, sir. He's still not entirely convinced of the veracity of the information being received, and is wary of being drawn into a trap."

"It'll be a moot point if we wait much longer!" Captain Frost said, turning away and starting to pace the open area between the two desks. "If the information is accurate and we hold off to verify, by the time we know anything the *Indomitable* will be sporting more firepower and able to easily fend us off. Do we wait until they decide to move against us, destroying every ship over Luna before obliterating the domes?"

"Erik, you have to see it from Holgerson's perspective. If we attack now and that cruiser is fully operational, then Luna is still left unprotected and we've gained nothing." Dex was trying to talk him down, but Meyers could see the captain was too passionate about this subject.

"Okay," he said, bringing the others to a halt. "I agree with you, Erik. We have to do something, or we risk falling into dangerous inertia. Frankly, I've been wanting to get most of our squads to Earth to assist the Coalition forces that are ignoring orders and fighting the invasion. Captain Fitz has pointed out that attempting to do so with the cruiser in orbit is inviting attack. The Syndicate could blow our ships out of the sky before they even got through the atmosphere."

"There was a mutiny," Frost said, throwing his arms in the air. "That means the *Indomitable* has to be operating against Syndicate orders. They wouldn't follow orders to protect a government they're currently rebelling against."

Meyers grinned and raised an eyebrow. "By that logic, we shouldn't fight them because they could be on our side. I know, they're still too dangerous to ignore. It's like petting a great white shark once and thinking it's tame. But there's the possibility." He turned his eyes to Dex. "Have we tried contacting Admiral Yumata, and asking his intentions?"

She shook her head slowly. "No, sir. They're still Syndicate Navy. Just because they didn't like the choice of commander doesn't mean they disagree with the Syndicate view of things. You know the Executive Committee will eventually see their way to accommodating the situation, and turn it to an advantage. You have to give them credit for not being locked into one mindset once they see proof they were wrong."

"Perhaps, but let's see what we can do in the meantime. If we get in early enough, perhaps we can talk Yumata into joining us. Independent of the Earth governments, working to form something better for the people living out here where life has different priorities."

"You'd actually work with them?" Frost was indignant now, and there was a simmering rage in his eyes. "They're still the same people who imprisoned two of our crews, that we know of. The same people who killed several members of the *Telemachus* crew, and were about to do the same to myself and my crew. The same people who blew up Interamnia because the colony there wouldn't submit to Syndicate rule. The same people who butchered citizens on

Mars and Deimos because of which part of Earth they came from."

Meyers rose and walked around his desk, hands held placatingly in front of him. "Erik, I didn't say I looked forward to working with them. But if we managed to sway that cruiser to support the Alliance, it would solidify our position in the system. Earth would have no choice but to accept us." As he got closer, he put a hand on the young captain's shoulder. "Put yourself in their place. When you served aboard a Coalition frigate, wouldn't you have followed the orders given to you by a superior officer? Even if you didn't agree with them?"

"I never would have killed innocent people!" Frost's eyes changed, though, as he really thought about it. Meyers didn't realize it, but the young captain was thinking about a conversation he'd had with his crew not too long ago on a similar subject. Discussing whether the actions of the ship could cast blame on everyone aboard.

"Well, I like to think I would never give the order to have them killed. But thankfully I've never been in a situation to have to consider it." He squeezed Frost's shoulder, then let go and turned to Dex. "Contact the *Waterloo*, let them know I plan to attempt communication with the *Indomitable* this evening. Let's say three hours from now. If they'd like to be on the line with me, I'm happy to have them."

Frost growled in frustration, and stomped out of the office. Dex looked after him a moment before turning back with an expression of apology. "I'll reach out to Commander Richtaus right away, sir."

He waved his hands, giving her permission to go after Frost. Perhaps she could talk him through the frustration that Meyers shared but couldn't express. He didn't particularly like the idea of working alongside a ship that had done such horrendous things, but the politician part of him had to acknowledge it made sense for the Alliance. If nothing else, it would give them time to build a better fleet to help take down the *Indomitable* later on if they suddenly decided to stop cooperating.

Returning to his desk, he keyed in the code for Rinde Brighton's private communication channel. Even though this technically had nothing to do with the situation on Earth, he felt honor bound to let the man know what he was planning to do. Perhaps they could even present a united front when he spoke with Admiral Yumata.

"Are you out of your mind?" Holgerson was looking at Meyers and Brighton on the screen, his expression tight. "The *Indomitable* sent soldiers onto my ship, gentlemen. They killed more than two dozen of my people, and tried to blow up the frigate and kill us all."

"Admiral, President Meyers and I are not enthused about the prospect, but if we can somehow sway the *Indomitable* to our side it will free up the *Waterloo* to assist with our efforts to push back the Syndicate invasion force." Brighton's words were calm, his deep voice projecting an inner strength that always seemed to reassure whoever he was talking to.

"They'd turn on us as soon as we showed them our back," Commander Richtaus blurted from the background. She stepped closer to the camera, growing larger on the wall screen as she bent over her admiral's shoulder. "The people on that ship have proven they have no honor, no sense of decency. They'd agree to cooperate just to make us lower our guards. Then they'd finish repairing their weapons and turn them on us while our attention was elsewhere."

Meyers smiled grimly. "I think we could count on you to always be watching, commander. Our own Captain Frost shares your distaste with the idea, and will never trust them. With both of you looking out, I feel confident we'd be more than prepared if they did attempt some kind of attack. Besides, isn't your Engineering department working with Dr. Francks on some great advancement in firepower using the fusion reactor we're letting you use?"

Holgerson grunted, turning to speak softly to Richtaus until she backed away. The woman was still grumbling, speaking angry words at her captain. "President Meyers, any such advancements are days away from testing, much less realistic use."

"But it is sound reasoning, isn't it?" Meyers pressed. "The science looks as if it will work, and the idea could increase the offensive capabilities of any ship with the Silva reactor?"

"Yes," Holgerson said, reluctantly. "If it passes testing, then it will give us a greater ability to inflict damage in a battle."

"That would seem to widen our advantage if we can hold off the *Indomitable* for a while, then. To me, it seems like negotiating with them has more advantages than disadvantages. Even if Admiral Yumata refuses to work with the Alliance, we've bought time for this new advancement of yours to be tested and put into action."

"You also give them time to get more of their railguns operational," Holgerson said. "Since receiving the first data burst, we have scanned the cruiser extensively. At this moment, I can say with confidence that at least half their railguns are nonoperational, along with most of their torpedo tubes. So yes, negotiating to gain time increases our offensive capabilities. But it also allows them to more than double their own."

Brighton sighed, and stepped in front of Meyers. He would be filling the screen on the *Waterloo*'s display. "Admiral, I concede that your observation has merit. It is something I have been considering since President Meyers approached me with his idea. But have we not seen enough bloodshed already? This war has claimed so many lives, and continues to claim more and more every day as the ground forces clash. If we have even the slightest chance of being able to turn our attention to stopping that, then I am convinced we must take it."

Holgerson stared at the screen for several moments, his jaw tightening. "Prime Minister Brighton, I have placed my ship at your command as head of the splinter government. It is my duty to follow your commands, sir."

"Admiral, it is *my* duty to look after the people." Brighton straightened, raising his chin as he looked directly at the camera built into the display. "We will attempt negotiations with the *Indomitable* in one hour. I will keep you apprised on the results."

Meyers sagged and leaned on his desk as the screen went black. "Thank you for backing me, Rinde. The last thing I need is to lose the support of the frigate just because I talk to the cruiser. That would be disastrous."

"Let us hope that trying to negotiate with the *Indomitable* isn't disastrous, my friend. You realize that a smart man will recognize we are reaching out because we have information from within the ship. From everything I've heard, Yumata is definitely a smart man."

"It's one of the many things I had to weigh in the balance. They'll guess it, but they won't have a way to know for sure. Hopefully our spy on board will be cautious, and realize their position is more tenuous."

"Hopefully," Brighton said, not sounding too certain.

Ten

Vegley was baffled by the message they'd just received. Yumata had called her into his office so they could watch it together, and then replayed it again. Both men on screen were older and dignified, representing the kind of politicians her parents had always moaned about never seeing anymore. Both of them asked to open negotiations, asked for Admiral Yumata to consider supporting the Alliance cause.

"Why would they want to negotiate?" Vegley asked. "We've been fighting against the Coalition for the last year."

"They know too much," Yumata said. "Somehow, they know that I have returned to the *Indomitable*, resumed my position of command. They know it was done against orders from the Syndicate committees. Otherwise, they would never have reached out in this way." He looked up from the holo display with a satisfied look. "We have a spy on board, commander. Reporting to Luna, apparently, though I confess I don't know which of the two governments."

"I'll have the Marines start sweeping the ship," Vegley said through gritted teeth. She couldn't believe there'd be a spy on *her* ship. Just when things seemed to be going so well, too.

"No," Yumata said, musingly. He stroked his upper lip in thought. "Leave them be for the moment. I imagine they've spilled our secrets by now. If the Alliance knows about our mutiny, then they must know about the situation with our armaments. I would have ordered an immediate attack in their position, but perhaps there is some reason they don't feel confident such a tactic would work."

Vegley sniffed in contempt. "I can't believe you use that name, sir. The Transport Guild is not fit to govern themselves, much less all off world settlements."

"President Meyers strikes me as quite competent, commander." Yumata rose from his chair, tucked his hands behind his back, and strode to look through one of the few real windows on the ship. Luna was passing through his view, and he considered it as he thought about the request. She wondered if he would really consider working alongside freighters. "I think we will allow them to send a delegation aboard, commander. No more than six, and no Marines."

"Sir! You can't seriously be considering this. The Executive Committee may have been foolish to put someone like Guildersen in charge, but the Syndicate is our home. I'm not the only person on board who would never turn our weapons on them."

"Nor would I," Yumata assured her. "However, I also feel that the Syndicate leadership has lost their way. Perhaps it happened long ago and it just took being away from the planet for so long to realize it. There is a better way to do things, but they refused to listen to any of my ideas while I was stuck on the planet. I don't believe our future lies with the Syndicate any longer."

Vegley stared at him, wondering for the first time what plans were running through his mind. She'd assumed that when the admiral returned to the ship, it would just mean putting things back to the way they had been before arriving at the homeworld. If he meant to do something else, she wasn't sure how she'd feel about being part of that. Had she made a mistake, joining in when Yumata suggested removing Guildersen from the ship?

"Don't worry, commander," he said, his eyes seeming to stare at her in the reflection of the glass. "I would never ask anyone on this ship to betray their home. I guarantee that we will never fire our weapons against the Syndicate unprovoked."

She nodded, unsure of how to feel. *What the hell?* she thought with resignation. *I'm already involved in this, might as well follow through.* "I'll send a message and make arrangements for our visitors, admiral. Should we accept their proposed time of tomorrow at midday?"

"No, I can't allow them to have their way too much. Tell them it will happen at sixteen hundred hours, or not at all. It gives us more time to continue with railgun installation and repairs. We must negotiate from a position of strength, if we are going to negotiate at all."

Vegley turned and left his office, entering the command deck to find the officers there glancing her way curiously. The communications lieutenant had been the first to receive the message, and sent it to the admiral's terminal. She wondered how much of it the man had seen before doing so, and how much of that had already spread across the command deck.

She passed communications, settling into a chair at the opposite end of the row of stations. She wanted privacy for the message she was sending, to prevent knowledge of the upcoming meeting spreading across the ship as gossip wildfire. In the overnight hours, she would leak the news to people she trusted. Discuss it with them, and make sure that when the word spread it did so with the appropriate tone. "It's just talking" she reassured herself.

Once the message was composed and sent, she pulled up reports on the ongoing repairs. They had nine functional railguns now, with one scheduled to be completed within the next hour. There were three work crews, with people walking on the hull at all hours. The defensive cannons, low caliber weapons that could fire faster but with less power than the railguns, were also being repaired. At the current moment, more than sixty percent of the ship was vulnerable to incoming fire. Torpedoes could slide through unopposed and tear holes in the cruiser, and there would be nothing they could do to stop it. She considered those smaller weapons the most important item on the repair lists, though it was more intensive work and there were fewer people qualified to do it.

Vegley cursed the *Waterloo* for surviving Ghost Squad's assault. If not for the frigate's return, the *Indomitable* would be free to target the pathetic freighters of the so-called Alliance and obliterate them. She'd like to see how smug and self-assured Meyers was when his only defenses were burning hunks of metal orbiting the moon. She was certain there wouldn't be any talks of cooperation then. More like pleas for mercy as they surrendered.

Would the Syndicate capitalize on such an event? Or would they still be too lost in what was happening on the planet below to even care. She vaguely wondered when any of the committees had spared more than a thought to the colonies, despite being responsible for creating most of them. When the mining colonies in the asteroid belt decided to govern themselves, no one on Earth had paid much attention. There was too much focus on the new cold war with the Coalition. She couldn't even remember the last time the

Syndicate had allowed people to leave Earth to join one of the colonies. Aside from the scientists that rotated through Mars and Deimos, that is.

She stiffened as she realized she was thinking much like Yumata now. Was there any point in trying to get back into the Syndicate's good graces? It was still the same government that had built the largest ship in the system, and then failed to provide the personnel and weaponry needed to make it as potent as it needed to be. The same government that had put an incompetent glutton in charge, and ignored any protests from those forced to suffer his bad leadership.

Perhaps the best solution would be to leave the Syndicate behind for good. It was a thought she'd have to give more consideration to.

ELEVEN

They stayed on the hilltop for more than an hour, sitting and watching the distant shimmering water as the sun fell to the horizon. Altan talked about their childhood trips, and Tuya told some stories about her first days on Luna, and it was with reluctance that they finally rose.

Altan brushed the dirt and grass from the pants of his white prison uniform, already hopelessly stained. "We should return to the others, let them know what we've seen."

"No," Tuya said. "We should walk toward the lake, and hope to arrive on the shore tomorrow. If we travel along it, we're sure to find a village soon. Fishermen will ferry us across the lake and save us from walking a hundred kilometers or more around it."

Her brother sighed and shook his head. "We can't just leave the others, Tuya. We know this land, we were born and grew up to it. They'll be lost. Could you bear it, knowing you left them to die without giving them the choice to come with us?"

"Yes," she said shortly. One look at his face was enough to make her relent, though. She wondered how he had held onto such compassion and optimism through everything he'd suffered over the last eight years. She also wondered how much of that she would share if she'd had the chance to spend those years with him. "Fine, we'll go back."

The journey seemed shorter this time. They almost jogged down the gentle slope of the hill, keeping their eyes on the ground for any obstacles they could see in the fading light. Twice Tuya spotted movement through the grass not far away, and wondered if it might be wild boar or foxes. Her stomach grumbled in hunger, and she was thinking of traps her father had showed her as a child. Hopefully, Altan remembered those lessons better than she, and they could manage to catch some food overnight or tomorrow.

When they arrived back at the area the shuttle had dropped them, there were only three figures waiting. Guildersen's large bulk was visible against the purple sky, still staring up as if expecting the shuttle to return for him at any moment. Abernathy was at his feet, sitting up with his head in his hands. The last person was the male prisoner, his eyes devoid of emotion as he stared listlessly into the distance.

"Where is the woman?" Tuya asked, gazing around to see if she might have hidden away in the tall grass.

"She ran away," Abernathy said, his voice muffled by his hands. She felt her lips tugging up in a smile, imagining the headache he must be experiencing after being hit with a stun bolt twice during the day. "Something about ants eating her from inside, and monsters chasing her. Who knows?"

Altan was looking conflicted, and Tuya put a hand on his arm. When he glanced over, she shook her head. "She was coming down from something potent, Alt. She could be five kilometers away by now, in any direction." He wasn't happy, but he nodded to show he understood.

"I think I know where we are," he said loudly enough for everyone to hear. "From the hill we could see water in the distance, and I'm fairly certain it's Lake Baikal. My sister and I grew up not far from there, and visited it often as kids. If I'm right, we can start walking south tomorrow and find a village on the shore in a day or two."

"No, we stay here." Guildersen's tone was that of a man who expected to be obeyed. It was almost a command, spoken in a way that said he was sure his ideas would overrule any other. "The pilot said he would alert the local authorities to our location, and we need to be here when they arrive."

Tuya snorted in disgust. "We've been on the ground for at least a couple of hours by now. You think they wouldn't have already come?"

"They won't leave me here," the officer said. "They wouldn't dare."

"You're delusional, Guildersen. If I were in their shoes, I'd only be too happy to let you rot away right here. Look around you! There's no one for at least twenty kilometers. This isn't an area that sees a lot of air traffic. Frankly, I doubt even the spy satellites both governments deny having are watching this barren part of the world." She held her arms out at her sides, turning in circles. "They didn't just happen to pick one of the few empty places left on this overpopulated rock."

Guildersen dragged his gaze away from the sky, turning angry eyes on her. "A traitor like your brother, or a filthy spy like yourself. That's who they would leave to rot. Even that idiot over there who keeps mumbling about someone called Mika. He's useless no matter where he came from. But I have contacts on the Executive Committee, Ms. Sansar. And this man is a member of the Military Committee. We are not the kind of men you leave in a field and forget."

Altan raised his hands and patted the air. "Alright, let's just drop it for now. We need to spend the night here, either way, so give it some thought. Tuya and I are leaving at dawn. If you wish to come, fine. If you don't, also fine."

Tuya grumbled under her breath as they worked to clear a space and pulled grass to bunch up on the ground. It wouldn't be the most comfortable night's sleep she'd ever had, but it would be better than nothing. It would be the first free night of sleep in weeks, which would more than compensate for having to sleep in the open.

She and Altan stretched out on their beds of grass, staring up at the stars. The man who was no longer moaning about Mika had finally risen to follow their lead, and was finishing his own bedding. Abernathy kept looking at them as if expecting someone else to make one for him, while Guildersen had returned to staring at the sky. She was sort of impressed that someone so round could stand for so long.

"Mom's going to kill me," Altan said quietly. "Showing up after not calling or writing for so many years."

"And dad's going to give you that look. The one that says you're a disappointment, but you're his child and he still loves you." They laughed, and Tuya could feel a tickle along her temple. "You know they're never going to let you leave again."

"Yeah. By the end of a week, mom will have found some nice village girl for me to marry."

"She'll already be picking out the names of your kids. And demanding at least three of them."

"Then she'll find some nice village boy willing to put up with you."

"And be picking out the names of my kids. Demanding at least three of them." She sighed, smiling so wide it hurt her cheeks. "I can't wait."

They were quiet for a while, lost in thought and viewing the vault of the heavens above. She felt fingers on her arm, a gentle touch as Altan traced the line of one of her scars. "Does it hurt?"

"All the time," she said quietly. "But it's getting better. I'm getting stronger." She didn't tell him that her entire body ached after their short trek to the hill and back. That she'd felt lightheaded when they returned, exhausted not only from the walk but from the gravity. Her brother had enough cares and worries to need another one heaped on his shoulders.

"Why did you do it? Get the implants."

Tuya bit her lip, not wanting to tell the story but also knowing there was no one else she'd rather share it with. "After you... well, died, or so we thought, I lost my way a little. If the universe could take away the thing I cared about most, I figured there was no point in treating it with respect. I thought I should just take what pleasure I could, while I was around to take it. About a month after remnants of the *Telemachus* were found, I left. I didn't tell mom or dad that I was going, I just waited until they were asleep and walked out. I hitched a ride to the spaceport, and hopped on the first ship going anywhere but there.

"I wanted to join up with a Guild ship, go into space like you did. I couldn't work alongside you, but I still wanted to honor your memory in some way." She sighed heavily. "It turns out getting to Luna was the easy part. A lot of stuff happened there, Alt, things I really don't like talking about. Along the way, I met some people who I trusted more than I should have. The implants were part of a plan to help me get into Aldrin dome, and I figured out too late that the cost was higher than I was willing to pay."

"Tuya, I'm so sorry. I never would have imagined you being in such a situation. I can't help but feel responsible." Altan sighed. "I shouldn't have always told you how great it was, working aboard a freighter. There were good times, but it was a lot of stress and hard work, too."

"I still would have wanted it," she assured him. "I still do, honestly. More than anything, now that I have you and you're safe, I wish I could get back to my ship."

"You will," he promised her. "Whatever it takes, you'll get back there."

When she woke the next morning, the first thing Tuya noticed was the ache deep in her bones. The increased weight of life in full gravity was going to prove to be more of a hindrance than she'd expected. Especially with her muscles still rebuilding themselves.

The second thing she noticed was that she and Altan were alone in the small clearing. She sat up quickly, looking around in every direction. She could feel a panic rising up inside, as she wondered if the shuttle pilot had called the local authorities after all. Had they come in the night and taken the other three? Why would they leave Tuya and Altan behind?

Faint voices to the west drew her attention. She rubbed sleep from her eyes as she crawled to her feet and walked toward them. People were arguing, and she thought that from the tones the one speaking the most was Guildersen. Abernathy's interjections seemed more timid, while also being peevish.

She managed to get a few yards away before they noticed her. Guildersen gave her a sneer, while Abernathy looked at her imploringly for some reason. "What's going on?" she asked.

The fat man waved his arm. "Oh, we were just noticing that you and your brother are absolute imbeciles. Tell me again how we're in southern Russia."

She looked at him in confusion, walking forward. That's when she noticed that the ground had been sloping gradually upwards. It dropped away suddenly a stride away from where she came to a stop, presenting a stunning view of a town not too far in the distance. A decidedly European-looking town. Except for the bomb craters and crumbling walls that were only half standing. It looked as if an army had swept through, destroying everything in their path.

"We're not far from the front," Guildersen said smugly. "We must be behind the Syndicate lines. We'll find a squadron of soldiers, and by nightfall I'll be back in charge of my ship while you and your brother will be locked away where you belong."

TWELVE

Mira maneuvered the freighter closer and closer to the *Waterloo*, until Erik heard the clunk of a secure connection to the docking port. He still couldn't believe he'd been talked into doing this when he was against the entire thing from the start. This idea of negotiating with the enemy was the worst kind of nonsense. He didn't see any future where the *Indomitable* could work alongside the Alliance or Coalition.

The man sitting in the normally vacant navigator station breathed a sigh of relief. "That was excellent piloting, Ms. Torv. I'm looking forward to our trip back to Luna." President Meyers unstrapped his restraints, stretching out his limbs as much as he could in the light gravity.

"I went extra gentle just for you, pres. Gotta take care of the important packages."

Meyers chuckled and patted her on the shoulder as he climbed out of his seat. He turned to look at Erik, presenting a calm smile. "Shall we head into the frigate, Captain Frost?"

Erik bit his lip to keep from picking up the argument that had been left unresolved before they boarded the *Vagabond* to leave Luna. He had tried to tell the Alliance leader that going into the heart of the enemy vessel himself was too much of a risk. Admiral Yumata could kill them as soon as they were aboard, and it was almost guaranteed to crush the Alliance before it really got started. Dex would step up to take the reins, but she didn't have the years of contacts and experience that Meyers did.

Instead, he buried his words deep down and followed Meyers through the corridor to the airlock. By the time the door on the other side cycled open, Captain Andrews and Admiral Holgerson were waiting for them. "President Meyers, it's a pleasure to welcome you aboard my ship," the admiral said, stepping forward to shake hands with both men.

"It's good to be here," Meyers said. "I have to admit this is the first time I've been aboard a frigate. I'm looking forward to seeing just how different it is from one of our freighters."

"I'll make sure we give you a tour once you return," Captain Andrews said. "Are you sure you want to go on this trip, sir? We can arrange a video feed so that your representative can attend in your place."

Erik snorted, glad to see that at least one other person shared his concerns. But Meyers only shook his head and smiled his politician smile. "This could be a very important meeting, captain. I feel it deserves my full attention and presence. If we are able to talk Admiral Yumata into joining us, or at the very least agreeing to a neutral position in the current events, then it is worth any amount of danger."

"I wish I could share your optimism," Holgerson said wryly, leading the way as the small group left the airlock antechamber and entered the ship's wide corridors. "Yumata is known to be one of the hard core Syndicate leaders. You don't get offered a spot on the Military Committee just because you worked hard, after all. My feeling is that he's allowing this farce only because it gives him more time to effect repairs to his ship."

Erik nodded, though he knew no one was looking at him. He trailed behind the other three men, hoping the *Waterloo*'s officers could talk sense to his president before it was too late. Even Dex hadn't been in support of Meyers personally attending this meeting, but she'd kept most of her reservations between the two of them. She said that she could tell when Meyers was dug in and wouldn't be budged.

"Gentlemen," the president said, "I appreciate your concerns. I'd be a fool if I didn't feel a bit of trepidation myself. The possibility of good is too great to let that stop me. If we can somehow remove the threat of the *Indomitable*, then we can turn our attention to helping the ground forces repel the Syndicate invasion. And getting Prime Minister Brighton on the ground to take control of the government and begin the process of fair elections."

By this time, they'd arrived at their destination. The docking bay was large, taking up six full decks of the frigate and stretching hundreds of meters in either direction. The admiral's gleaming white shuttle was waiting in the middle of the deck, with a pilot standing respectfully at the bottom of the ramp. Commander Richtaus was also waiting, along with Dr. Francks.

The physicist hurried forward. "President Meyers. It is good to see you, sir. We have been doing wonderful work here with the new reactor over the last week, and I have a quite a few projects to update you on. For instance, we've found a way of using the increased energy production to change the resonant vibration around the ship. We feel that if we can fine tune this fascinating new..."

"Thank you, doctor." Mags stepped forward and inserted herself in front of the physicist. "The shuttle is ready to go," she said to Admiral Holgerson.

Erik shared a nod with her. The woman had a prickly attitude, but he'd come to respect her in the time since he'd first met her. She knew her ship well, and always kept the crew's well-being front and center in any decision she had to consider. He was glad she'd be accompanying them.

The final member of the foursome making the trip to the cruiser exited the shuttle. Captain Tom Fitz had transferred over to the frigate earlier in the day, wanting to have plenty of time for his preparations. He was dressed in the new uniform of the Alliance military, gray shirt tucked into black pants with red stripes on each shoulder to show his rank. The icon of a hand drawing back a bow was in red stitching over his heart. "Everything is ready, sir," he said to Meyers.

"Wonderful. We should depart. I don't want to be late for our meeting, and set a bad precedent before we've even started."

He and Erik shared farewell handshakes with Andrews and Holgerson, then followed Mags into the shuttle. It was a richly appointed ship, with real leather seats almost wide enough for two people to share. There were six of them, leaving two empty when the group had settled in. Even though Admiral Yumata had allowed six people to visit the cruiser, Meyers had decided to only use three spots for Alliance representatives. He'd offered the other three for the Coalition, but only Lieutenant Commander Richtaus had been selected.

The shuttle ride was smooth, a forty minute trip from the *Waterloo* in orbit around Luna to the *Indomitable* still in orbit over Hong Kong. Erik kept the display attached to his seat on a view of Earth as they got closer. It was nighttime over this part of the planet, and he stared at the millions of twinkling lights in wonder. He had wispy memories of living in a tightly packed town as a kid, but a decade and a half in space had made him more accustomed to the lightly populated domes and colonies.

"We've been authorized to land in Bay Two," the pilot said over the intercom as they approached the cruiser. Erik forced his attention away from the planet, changing the view on his display to show the massive ship they were approaching. It was hard to tell which weapons he could see were functional or just mocked up to look that way. He hated knowing that the ship had been vulnerable for so long, and they'd been held back from attacking because they never realized it. This whole situation could have ended a week earlier. But, nothing was ever that simple.

He felt slight turbulence as the shuttle passed through an ion barrier, and then a gentle thump as they settled to the decking. The whine of the door opening was the signal for all four to unstrap and stand. Without discussing it, they exited the shuttle in an unconscious order of precedence. President Meyers led the way, with Commander Richtaus behind, followed by Erik and then Tom.

A woman was waiting at the bottom of the ramp, with a tight smile on her face. Two Marines flanked her, with stun pistols in their hands. Erik stiffened when he saw them, convinced they really had stepped into a trap. Once the woman had looked over each person exiting the ship, she waved to the Marines and they hurried up the ramp and into the shuttle. Then she stepped forward to greet them. "Welcome to the *Indomitable*. I am Commander Vegley, XO."

"Commander, it is a pleasure to make your acquaintance." Meyers reached out to shake her hand. "Your Marines are not necessary, I assure you. There are only four of us, along with the shuttle pilot."

"Standard security sweep," Vegley said. "Forgive me, President Meyers, but I find it hard to trust that this isn't some kind of trap."

You and me both, Erik thought. He shared a look with Tom, both of them wondering if they should have pushed harder to keep Meyers from being here. It was especially weird for them, returning to a ship that had imprisoned them not too long ago. Erik had only been there for several days, but Tom had endured seven years. He was surprised the man had agreed to come along at all.

"You're welcome to scan it," Meyers said. "Your people will find nothing amiss. May I introduce you to the rest of our party? This is Lieutenant Commander Richtaus, XO of the *Waterloo*. Captain Erik Frost, of the *Vagabond*. And Captain Tom Fitz, the commander of the Alliance military."

Vegley sniffed after the introductions. "Yes, I've heard a few of those names before." She looked at Erik and Tom with a brief sneer, then turned her attention back to Meyers. She ignored Mags completely. "Admiral Yumata is waiting in his office. Follow me, please."

As they left the bay, another pair of Marines fell in behind the group. Erik glanced back at them uncertainly, but was glad to see the stun batons they carried were strapped to their thighs. He hoped the soldiers were there just to make sure no one got lost. Walking through the corridors was like returning to a nightmare. He'd seen little of the ship on his last visit, but every corridor had the same look and feel of those he'd run through trying to get back to his ship. He thought of the Syndicate Marines he'd helped kill, and wondered if they had friends on board that might want a little revenge.

When Vegley stopped at a door and waved for them to enter, his body tensed in anticipation. A large part of him was expecting to see a firing squad just inside, and he didn't relax until he entered to find only a single man waiting for them. Admiral Yumata looked immaculate in his black uniform, with eight red slashes over his heart for his rank. His face was smooth and expressionless, the mask of a man accustomed to hiding whatever he might be feeling inside.

"President Meyers," the admiral said, holding out a hand toward a table set up with eight chairs. "Please, take a seat. There is water on the table. If anyone would like other refreshment, don't hesitate to ask."

Meyers selected his seat, and Erik sat to one side while Mags took the seat on the other side. Tom looked at the chairs, and then leaned against the wall behind Meyers instead. It was a spot where he could view every occupant of the table without having to move his head. Yumata noticed, but said nothing as he sat across from Meyers. Vegley sat beside him, leaving the Marines outside the door.

"Before we begin," Yumata said softly. "I would like to clarify one thing. While I may have disobeyed orders to reclaim my command of this ship, that does not mean I have turned my back on my government."

"I would never accuse you of that," Meyers said. "I am merely hoping we can discuss the current situation, calmly and rationally. I'm confident we can agree to many things. Starting with the need for stability. Nothing good has come of this flare up between the Syndicate and the Coalition."

"Oh, I don't know." Vegley spoke with a one-sided smile. "We've destroyed all but one Coalition warship."

Mags grunted, gritting her teeth and giving a snarling smile. "You destroyed two. Technically, our own traitorous government destroyed the other three while you sat here on your ass and watched."

"Ladies, please. Let's be civil." Meyers didn't sound as if he minded the verbal sparring, though. Erik wondered if it was a political tactic. He also noticed that neither Meyers nor Yumata glanced at the commanders while they traded barbs. "Admiral, what would it take for you to agree not to fight my ships if we land troops to help against the invasion forces on Earth?"

"President Meyers, allowing such a thing would be akin to betraying my country. I don't agree with their idea of how to run this ship, but I find no fault with their invasion. As the good Commander Richtaus has said, her own government is corrupt and working with my government. That would suggest they agree that the Syndicate is the better option."

"Hardly," Mags said. Meyers laid a hand on her arm. She jerked it away, but kept her silence.

"Innocent people are being killed and left homeless because of that invasion," Meyers said. "Millions more are at risk once the Syndicate forces reach the more heavily populated regions of western and northern Europe. Will you take that on your conscience?"

"It is not on my conscience at all," Yumata replied. "I do not command the ground forces, nor do I make the decisions of how to use them. One could say that the fault for those deaths is on Coalition hands. Had their commanders not gone against orders from the prime minister, our Syndicate army would still be marching forward without firing a shot."

Erik wondered how much longer this was going to last. It was already clear to him that the *Indomitable*'s leader wasn't going to accede to anything that Meyers had hoped for. They definitely weren't going to join with the Alliance.

"Can we at least make an agreement that our ships will not fire on each other, as long as neither side tries to get to the surface?" Meyers seemed to be grasping at straws, but Erik couldn't see any change in his tone or expression.

Yumata considered that proposal, glancing at his XO before responding. "I would be amenable to such an agreement. As long as we stipulate that neither side can fire on the planet, as well."

Mags shifted, and Erik could tell she wasn't happy with the way this was going. Meyers seemed to not notice, however. "Would you agree to withdraw from orbit? You could join our ships over Luna, or perhaps take a position an equal distance from Earth at another point."

Yumata shook his head. "That I can't agree to. Our position here was ordered by the Executive Committee. Until I have an opportunity to speak with them and explain my reasoning for returning to command, I must abide by that order."

Erik zoned out as the Meyers and Yumata continued going back and forth. At one point, Yumata offered to negotiate with his government on behalf of the Colonial Alliance, but Meyers turned him down with a sardonic smile. Even Mags had finally sat back and folded her arms to signal that she was checked out, as the two leaders continued to lob proposals and denials at each other.

Two hours after entering the office, everyone stood and the conference came to an end. Meyers and Yumata shook hands, smiling at each other while both men's eyes remained hard. Erik knew this was the perfect time to spring a trap, right when his group would be most relaxed. He kept expecting the doors to slide open as Marines filled the room.

Vegley led them back to Bay Two, with the same two Marines trailing the group. Tom seemed just as surprised when they marched up the ramp and into the shuttle without incident. He shrugged at Erik before taking a comfortable seat. Even Mags seemed a little confused as the door closed and the shuttle lifted from the deck to begin the return flight.

"Well, that was pretty pointless," Erik said aloud.

"Quite the contrary," Meyers said. "We learned a great deal that we didn't know before."

"Such as?" Mags asked, eyebrows raised.

"For one, they have no intention of holding to the agreement we just signed for our ships to not attack each other." Meyers glared at the display in front of him, showing the hull of the *Indomitable* as they glided past on the return trip to the frigate. "I don't know what they're planning, but it's bigger than the war between Earth governments."

THIRTEEN

The officer's lounge was quiet, with only a handful of people occupying tables. No one was sitting at the bar itself, as she wiped down glasses and stacked them beneath the counter. Mabel Harris bit her lip, watching the door and hoping someone she knew had been on the command deck that day would enter. She'd spent the hour before her shift trying to get into Bay Two, unsuccessfully. Even flirting with a beefy female marine had gotten her nothing but a lot of bad breath blown in her face when the woman tried to kiss her.

She hadn't started out intending to become a spy. History was her true love, especially early twentieth century history. As a kid, she could sit in front of a display for hours watching documentaries about mobsters or the two world wars. One of her favorite games was to imagine herself as one of the people on the screen, thinking of small changes she could have made to history to have her present turn out better than it had.

Now she only thought of the small changes that had put her in this position. If her scholarship hadn't been canceled, she never would have joined the Syndicate Navy in pursuit of their college fund.

If the recruiter hadn't selected her to tend bars instead of working with the naval historians, she never would have been sent out to join the *Indomitable*.

If Tuya Sansar, using the name Delta Smith, hadn't been selected as her roommate, she never would have been convinced that she should resume using the communication equipment an old colleague had given her when he finally retired.

At the time, she'd thought it a lark to find out she'd been working beside a Coalition spy for most of a year as they served drinks to the top brass on the Syndicate's main base. Pete told her he'd accepted the job because it offered a couple thousand extra credits each year. He'd send little tidbits he overheard in the officer's club, and in return money would be left in his digital account a few days later. He swore he never passed on anything too sensitive.

Mabel's story about losing the scholarship only days before beginning her final year at the university had affected him. He told her about his activities two days before leaving the base, knowing that she could turn him in if he'd read her wrong. She'd been intrigued, though, thinking about the credits she could earn. At the time, there'd been almost three years of naval service left before she qualified for any college assistance. Pete thought she could make enough to fund her final year in half that time, even by sending small bits that wouldn't harm the Syndicate efforts.

Her first broadcast had been the most nerve-wracking. She turned on the equipment, calibrated the signal as Pete had instructed, and then typed in the information she'd picked up that day about some personnel changes on the orbital station. When she tapped the button to send the data, sweat was streaming down her face and soaking her shirt. The rest of that night, she huddled in pitch black quarters convinced a security team would break down her door at any moment to arrest her.

When four hundred credits arrived in her account several days later, she knew she'd keep transmitting information. She was cautious, though, always waiting at least a few weeks before broadcasting again and never sticking to the same schedule. She'd carry the equipment out of the base and hike deep into a park before sending it, or find a crowded shopping center and set up in an out of the way place. Never from her quarters after that first time.

After arriving on the *Indomitable*, she thought her extracurricular activity was at an end. The ship was so large and powerful that she felt convinced they would crush any opposition they faced. Clearly the Syndicate would be on the winning side, and she couldn't risk being caught now. Then her roommate, a woman she'd grown to know and secretly love, was exposed as a Guild operative and implant freak. Mabel knew she should have shared everyone else's disgust and revulsion, but she couldn't. The woman she'd known as Delta had been as grounded and rational as anyone she'd ever known. More than most of them, in fact.

By the time they arrived at Earth, barely scraping through two short encounters with the Coalition fleet, she'd almost convinced herself to share information again. It took days of arguing with herself before she sent the first data burst, targeting the newly arrived *Waterloo* since signals away from Earth would have less chance of detection. The first tidbits she shared were about weapons that weren't working, something she'd overheard when a lieutenant from Engineering sat at the bar and spilled out his worries and stresses. She'd felt that old fear after sending the information the first time, but again no one seemed to know it had happened.

When she learned of Admiral Yumata's return, she'd been as happy as everyone else on board. Having to deal with Captain Guildersen had been a dreadful chore from the first moment she stepped aboard the cruiser, and she was quite happy to have him gone. Learning that Tuya Sansar had been released from her cell and sent to Earth was a kick in the gut. She'd found out about the woman's brother at the same time, though, and understanding that motivation made her love Tuya even more.

Mabel hadn't hesitated to send that data burst as soon as her shift was over, hoping someone on the Coalition ship would be able to help Tuya. Maybe even rescue her once she was on the ground. That night, she'd dreamed of being on Earth, seeing Tuya across a crowded room and running toward her. They were both laughing, happy to see each other, but never got any closer. Every step she took seemed as insubstantial as air. She'd woken from the dream with a twisted feeling in her chest, and called in sick for that evening's shift.

Tonight she was back behind the bar, hoping she'd hear something about the conference Admiral Yumata had been in with the president of the Alliance. It was an intriguing new government, and she thought about how such movements had led to great things in the past. The United States, Australia, Canada; all had started out as colonies, and grown to become great independent entities in their own right.

The door slid open, and a familiar face walked into the lounge. The lieutenant was around her age, in his late twenties, with few friends on board. After a few nights at the bar, he'd returned after almost every shift to grab a cocktail and chat with her. She gave him the attention he desired and couldn't seem to find anywhere else.

"Lieutenant Nelson. It's good to see you again, sir." Mabel smiled at him, walking over and pulling out the bottles she'd need to make a classic gin fizz. She'd been practicing it for a few days, hoping someone would order it. Nelson didn't care what he drank, so she always tested her newest concoctions on him.

"Hi, Mabel. It was a tough shift, so I'm hoping you have something good for me tonight."

She winked as she poured a liberal amount of gin into the metal shaker. "I think you'll enjoy this one. A little sweet, with a tartness to counterbalance. Very popular in the United States in the early 1900s, especially in New Orleans. Great things came out of that city; jazz, beignets, Mardi Gras, and gin fizzes." She gave the tumbler a last shake, pouring the contents into a chilled glass and then setting it in front of him.

Nelson took a sip, savoring the flavor before nodding in appreciation. "That's really good stuff. You should make it a part of the permanent menu."

"If they'd let me make changes, I would." Mabel grabbed a rag and started to wipe her counter. "So what's got you stressed tonight?"

"Aw, it's this crap with the Alliance people. Commander Vegley's been in a bad mood all day, and she's been a little snappish since that meeting ended. She blames me for people on the ship finding out about it before the admiral wanted them to. But all I did was my job! I get a message, I send it to where it needs to go."

"That sounds like a tough situation." She leaned in to put her elbows on the bar. "They should know how hard it is to keep information secret on a ship like this."

"Exactly! Like this stuff about the admiral's special shipment from Earth. You can't blame me if that gets out when the people in the cargo bay are going to know about it."

"Of course not, sir. It's not your fault when other people talk about things like that. A special shipment sounds like the kind of juicy gossip the boys and girls in the cargo bay can't help but talk about."

Nelson nodded, taking a big gulp of the drink. "Yeah, especially when they open it and find the hydroponics equipment inside. And the habitat shelter grids. That's exactly the kind of thing that's going to make people curious, and they can't help but talk about it." He shook his head, draining the last of the gin fizz. "I just know I'm going to get glared at again tomorrow, and the commander will be blaming me for spreading information. It's just so unfair."

Mabel reached out and put her hand on his. "It is totally unfair, lieutenant. You don't deserve any of that."

"Thanks," he said, gulping as he looked at her hand on his. She felt bad for the kid, but he was her biggest source of information. She had to keep working him to get more of it. "Say, would you, uh, like to meet me in the mess tomorrow night?" Nelson glanced up with nervous eyes that darted away as soon as they met hers.

"I'd like that," she said, hoping she could think of a nice way to get out of it.

As soon as her shift was over, Mabel hurried through the ship. She'd explored as much as she could in her early days after arriving on one of the Syndicate frigates, and found a perfect spot where she could be alone and not worry about some random crewperson stumbling upon her. It was a maintenance tunnel junction, far on the edges of the ship where nothing important passed through.

Her communication gear was stashed there, wrapped in a grease stained cloth and tucked behind conduits and wiring. She knew it wasn't the best place for it, but better it be discovered there than in her quarters. At least there was nothing that could tie it to her if it were found. The cloth had been soaked in a solvent that ate away fingerprints and genetic traces. She was always careful not to handle it much when she needed to use the gear.

Once she reached the hatch she used to access the tunnels, Mabel looked up and down the corridor to make sure she was alone. The panel was attached with magnetic locks that she'd bypassed in her first week on the ship. With a light touch on each corner, it popped off in her hands. She shimmied into the tunnel, pulling the panel closed after her. It took less than half a minute.

Crawling to the junction in the tight space was the hardest part. She'd grown up in a small town, accustomed to wide open spaces, and hated to admit that she felt claustrophobic even in the lifts that she avoided in favor of the stairs. The journey was only a few hundred meters, and she crawled as quickly as possible every time to reach the more spacious area.

The junction was still tight, but large enough that she could sit up straight and stretch her legs out. She reached between the conduits, grasped the wrapped box, and pulled it out. She tossed the astringent-smelling cloth aside quickly, already feeling a slight burning on her fingertips, and then opened the steel box. The area inside was large enough to hold two bottles of liquor from the bar, but it was stuffed with electronics. A small screen filled the lid, with half a dozen wires that could connect to the circuit boards in the main compartment. There was also a thick wire that she could pull out and attach to any surface. That was the antenna that sent the data burst.

Mabel hurriedly connected all the leads to activate the equipment, happy to see the screen light up and come to life. Once the keyboard was visible, she typed out the message detailing everything the lieutenant had told her at the bar. It wasn't much, but she felt it was important for some reason. Hopefully, whoever was getting her messages would know what it could mean.

She'd wondered at first if anyone were receiving, wishing the unit would get confirmations even as she knew that would only increase the danger and likelihood of getting caught. The meeting that had occurred with the Alliance president would seem to verify that someone was seeing her data bursts, though. Without the information she had sent, there was no reason to think Admiral Yumata could be reasoned with.

With the message ready, she pressed the key to encrypt the data, compress it, and then send it out to the designated location. It was a quick process, but Mabel felt like it was taking forever as she watched the progress bar fill the screen. As soon as confirmation of transmission appeared, she shut the unit down and started to disconnect everything. She had to be sure the device was fully powered down so it wouldn't be detected by random security sweeps that might be checking for unregistered electronics.

She wrapped the cloth around the box, stuffed it back into the nest of conduits and cables, and then rubbed her hands against her trousers to get rid of the burning feel. As she crawled back through the tunnels, she thought about her waiting bunk. She was still exhausted after her restless night of bad dreams, and hoped to get a good six hours to help make up for that. Then it was back to work tomorrow to see if Nelson showed up with more information snippets that she could share.

Mabel popped the panel loose, pushed it aside, and crawled out of the maintenance tunnel. After she put the panel back on, making sure it was secured well enough to not fall off, she straightened and brushed her clothes to get rid of any dust she might have picked up.

"It appears you were correct, commander. We will have to give the lieutenant a few lessons on how to not talk so much outside the bridge."

Mabel stiffened at the voice, her hands clenching into fists. Even though she'd never seen the man, she knew it was Admiral Yumata. No one else could speak with such a natural tone of command. She turned to face him, standing a few meters down the corridor with Commander Vegley at his side. Four Marines were behind them, and when she glanced over her shoulder she found the remainder of the squad there. The corridor was covered, and there was nowhere to run.

"This is the spy, sir," Vegley said through a happy smile. "It's almost too much of a cliché, the bartender selling secrets."

Yumata stepped forward, examining her. "Now, young woman, you will show us how you send these messages. I should like to use your little device for myself."

FOURTEEN

Tuya urged everyone to hold back and observe the distant town for at least a few hours, but Guildersen and Abernathy were feeling renewed energy at the thought of being so close to their own military forces. The other male prisoner, who finally told them his name was Robbins and that he was a crewman in Engineering, voiced his own desire to find friendly faces.

She and Altan watched the other three stomp through the tall grass, sliding and half jumping down the slope. "This is so stupid," Tuya said. "That's a bombed out town. There's nothing to say which side bombed it, or how long ago it was done. We could be five kilometers from the front or five hundred."

Altan only shrugged, pulling her hand to follow as he took the first step to begin the descent. "Those three know a lot more about what's going on than either of us. I didn't even realize there was an invasion until this morning."

"Neither did I, but that still doesn't mean we should follow them headlong into whatever they want to do. Think about it, Alt. Do we even want to be around if they find Syndicate forces? We'll end up back in jail."

"We face that threat as long as we're in Syndicate territory. Do you think they'll ever stop looking for us once word is out that we managed to escape the *Indomitable*? At least if we tag along, we'll have warning of when we're getting close to capture so that we can get away from it."

She shook her head in disagreement, but followed her brother down the graveled slope. Within ten minutes, everyone was on better ground. Guildersen moved faster than she would expect from someone who weighed easily three times as much as she did. He had to feel the same pressure from increased gravity, but didn't show signs of it so far.

Abernathy had turned into a chatterbox, talking brightly about the many changes he was going to propose as soon as he returned to Hong Kong. "..and we're definitely going to have to start sending protective squads with committee members who leave Earth. This sort of thing just must not happen again. Can you imagine the panic my shareholders must be going through right now, worrying that I might not return to my company?"

Tuya sniffed, wondering how many of those shareholders were hoping that didn't happen. He was the sort of man she imagined had inherited a company instead of building it himself. More than likely, there was a team of executives who ran the company for him and did their best to keep him from screwing things up.

When she was younger, she had always complained about living in a small village. She'd yearned to be in a big city where the centers of power were found. One of the games her schoolmates used to play was "Board Meeting", where they'd form a circle, vote for someone as CEO, and then pretend to be running the largest company in the world. Looking back, she was glad it had never become anything more than a game. She would hate to be like Abernathy.

By midmorning, they were nearing the town. A small stream crossed their path, and everyone agreed to stop and drink their fill. It had been more than twelve hours since any of them had anything to eat or drink, and they were beginning to feel the effects. Tuya was so thirsty that she didn't think about what could be in the water until she slurped down three cupped handfuls. As long as there wasn't an industrial site upstream, they should be okay. She hoped.

Guildersen was too eager to reach the town, and after no more than a minute he was already walking away again. Abernathy followed along like a loyal little puppy barking at his master's heels. Robbins cast a glance at them, but swallowed down a few more handfuls of water before racing to catch up.

"We should turn away," Tuya said once they were alone. "We're close enough that we'd be hearing noises if that town was still occupied. It's totally silent."

"That's why we need to keep going," Altan replied. "We need food, Tuya. We aren't going to be able to run very far if we're too weak to walk in a few days. There should be supplies in that town, hopefully enough for us to fill a sack or something."

She chewed on her lip, hating that her brother was making such good sense. After a few more drinks of water, wishing they had a canteen or bottle to save some for later, she stood and trudged through the stream to continue on toward the town. Altan was right behind her, laughing when he saw a cloud of butterflies take to the air ahead of them. The other three men had walked right through the field of flowers the insects were inhabiting.

Once again, she wished she could feel the same optimism as her brother. She wondered if she had been the same way when she was younger, in the years before she thought her brother dead. That event had driven her to dark places, but she couldn't help but think that even before then she'd always been more inclined to pessimism than Altan. Much like their parents; their mother was always happy and cheerful, while their father was more taciturn and abrupt.

The town was larger than it had looked from a distance. There were at least a couple of dozen businesses, along with a few hundred houses. They all sat on a perfectly square grid of streets, telling Tuya the town was no more than a hundred years old and probably less. Built when orderly city planning became more important than fitting into the landscape around the area.

The main road passed through the center of the town, continuing northwest and southeast until it disappeared in the distance. Tuya and Altan stood in the middle of it looking both directions for any movement. Guildersen and Abernathy had barged into the first store they found, pushing through the crumbling brick wall where it looked as if a grenade had exploded from inside. Robbins straddled the groups, standing just outside the store and glancing back at the brother and sister now and then as if reassuring himself they were still there.

"Ah hah!" Guildersen shouted, exiting the store with two dented cans held high. "There is still food here. You prisoners should eat. I wouldn't want anyone to think I mistreated you when I turn you over to the soldiers." His sneering smile was almost enough to make her storm across and punch it off his face, but the thought of food was more interesting to her at that moment.

Altan led her into the store, pushing past Guildersen when the fat man refused to budge and make their entry easier. The officer only chuckled when she sneered at him, the sound turning to an indignant yelp when she took the opportunity to grab a roll of fat and twist as hard as she could. Not as hard as she would have liked, or as hard as she would have been capable of when she still had her implants.

The interior of the store was a mess, with concrete blocks from the roof littering the ground. Shelves had been knocked aside either by the grenade blast or collapsing ceiling, with cans and jars scattered across the ground. Few of the glass jars had survived, and most of them were shattered with their contents now rotting in the open air.

"This wasn't very recent," Altan said quietly, as he nudged a moldy shriveled pickle with his flimsy prison shoe. "I'd say at least a week, maybe two."

"Good, that means any soldiers are long gone." Tuya turned her attention to the aluminum cans, looking for those with no holes to release the vacuum seal. As she set them aside in two piles, she let out a happy cry.

"What is it?" Altan asked, taking quick steps to stand behind her. She held up two plastic pouches, each showing a picture of a fish on the front. Both pouches were still sealed, the food inside still good. "Score," he said, smiling down at her as he took the pouches.

They continued to dig through the debris in the store, and soon had an impressive stack of cans and pouches that were mostly undamaged. Altan even managed to find a burlap sack in the back of the store, where deliveries were received. They stuffed almost everything into the sack, throwing in three bottles of water they'd managed to find. Then the sack was stuffed in a corner of the room, and they piled debris over and around it. Altan kicked dirt and dust around until it looked undisturbed.

As they exited the store into the glare of a summer sun directly above them, Tuya held out five cans of vegetables and fruit. "I guess this will have to do for lunch," she said, trying to sound dejected at not finding more. Abernathy and Guildersen already had empty cans sitting beside them, so she handed one to Robbins and kept the others for herself and Altan. The crewman gave her a grateful look, pulling the tab and twisting the lid open.

While they ate, Guildersen yelled for any survivors to show themselves. The man had a great set of lungs, she had to admit. His voice echoed through the town, and she felt sure anyone huddled in a house on the outskirts could hear him. He kept at it for five minutes, before letting out a disgusted growl and dropping to sit on the road with the others. Tuya's feet and legs were aching from the morning walk, and she knew the others had to be feeling the same. Except for Abernathy, the only one among them accustomed to Earth's gravity. And yet, he looked the most exhausted of them all.

"We'll search the houses," Guildersen pronounced. "There must be tablets here, or some other kind of communication devices. I will coordinate the searches from here, and you are to report back to me as soon as you find anything."

Tuya raised her eyebrow as he spoke, wondering if he really thought they'd all hop to his every command. Robbins did, jumping to his feet and heading in the indicated direction, but she and Altan remained seated. Guildersen turned to them with a scowl. "You prisoners will do as you're told, unless you want to end up in a dark hole once we're back in civilization. I promise you that I can make the rest of your lives long and painful if you push me."

Altan shook his head when Tuya opened her mouth, upending his can of apricots to drink the last of the juice. He rose and pulled her up with him, but walked in a different direction than Guildersen was pointing for them to go. "Why did you stop me?" she asked. "We're not really going to let that pig order us around like peons, are we?"

"We are when we want the same thing." Altan smiled at her, his eyes twinkling. "I want to find a way to communicate as much as he does, just with different people. If we can find a working tablet or display, then we can try to get in contact with the *Vagabond* or Luna and let them know where we are."

"Oh," she said simply, rolling her eyes at her own stupidity. Tuya knew she let her anger override her sense too often, and it was nice to have Altan back to keep her in check. The first house they encountered was empty, the door standing open and only the largest furniture remaining inside. There was a wall display in the main room, but no matter where they tapped on the screen it refused to light up.

"It looks like the people here had warning," Altan said. "Enough to take their smaller possessions and flee. So we must be far enough from the border that they weren't swept in the first surprise attacks."

"Look at this," Tuya called, waving for him to join her beside the food storage device. There was a rotten smell emanating from within, but her attention was focused on a pad of paper magnetically attached to the side. On the top was an advertisement for a business, one that she assumed was local. "If this is where we are, then we must have been looking at the Adriatic Sea yesterday."

"Great, so I was only off by about five thousand kilometers," Altan said, groaning and raking his fingers through his hair. "I was seeing what I wanted to see."

"Well, it's not like either of us know the planet all that well, Alt. It's been years since we were here, and we never really travelled as kids. The only thing I know about places beyond Mongolia are things I saw in pictures or entertainment shows."

"Still, it was a stupid mistake. I let my hopes lead me into jumping to conclusions." He reached over and hugged her with one arm. "I'm glad you found this, sis. At least now we can make better plans on how to get away from here when we need to."

"Oh?" She looked at him with a sardonic smile. "I'm glad you think so. I couldn't tell you where we are in relation to anything important. I just know the border between the Syndicate and Coalition territories should be a few hundred kilometers east of here."

"We also know why these people had the time to get out of here," he pointed out. "It would have taken days for an invasion force to reach this town, unless they invaded from the sea. So, the good news is we should be at least a few days from the front, but the bad news is that we're deep in Syndicate occupied territory."

Tuya considered that for a while, trying to picture a map of Europe and Asia in her head. She thought there might be a big spaceport not far away. Relatively, since it would still be a few hundred kilometers. "Do you remember when I was seven or eight, and everyone was making a big deal about Venice flooding?"

Altan tapped a finger on his lips and nodded. "Yeah, it was sad to see such an old city under a foot of water. And then it never receded. I remember the Syndicate committees crowing about how the Coalition couldn't even spare the resources to build a jetty to hold back the waters of the Mediterranean and save the historic islands."

"What I remember most was the scientists claiming the new spaceport built on the edge of the mainland could have been responsible in some way. Or maybe it took the funds that were going to be used for the protective dike."

"Well, I don't know if that was true or just Syndicate propaganda. But I think I know where you're going with this. That spaceport became one of the busiest hubs, and the place that supplied Aldrin and the orbital station. Most of the fleet supplies shipped through there, as well."

"And now it's probably in enemy hands. But there should still be some ships there, don't you think? Or at least advanced communications gear that would allow us to get in contact with Erik."

They discussed it as they continued to search the houses along the street. Tuya was feeling real excitement for the idea, even as Altan cautioned her that it was a long trip with unknown complications. The spaceport near the ruins of Venice was at least a hundred kilometers away, and twice as far when you factored in having to travel around the coast. Tuya was convinced they could find a boat somewhere, which would make the trip faster and easier.

The power in the town had apparently been shut off deliberately before the invasion forces arrived, or been cut by those soldiers as they swept through. Displays in every house remained dark, and the one tablet they found had a dead battery. Tuya still tucked it away in the small of her back, in case they found a way to charge it somewhere and it turned out to be useful. Food was spoiled or rotten, though they did manage to grab a few more vacuum sealed cans along the way.

Guildersen started bellowing for them halfway through the search, but Tuya and Altan ignored him. She even moved slower, thinking about how irritated he must be getting with them. By the time they returned to the street outside the grocery store, the officer's face was red and his jowls were shaking.

"I've been calling you for half an hour. If you can't do as you're told, I'll put you in restraints myself and leave you behind."

"Good luck with that," Tuya said, dropping a few cans of food in front of Robbins. The crewman was looking worn out, sitting with his arms wrapped around his knees and his head buried. He looked up long enough to smile at her, and she wondered why she cared about making sure he had a share of everything.

"The power to this town has been turned off," Guildersen continued, ignoring her. "I've decided that we will walk west, and see if we can catch up with the invasion forces or some of the soldiers left behind to secure our new territory."

"You can do whatever you want," Tuya said, dropping to sit with her back against a short stretch of undamaged wall. "My brother and I are going to stay here for the night, and sleep in a real bed." Altan nodded, sliding down next to her. "Then we'll decide where we want to go in the morning."

Guildersen marched over, sneering at them. "You will do as I command, prisoners. You don't get a vote in the matter."

"Captain, you need to learn to listen to good advice when it's offered." Altan's voice was calm, reasonable and reassuring. "I know you have to be feeling the effects of increased gravity like the rest of us. A night of good sleep, a bit more food in our bellies, and we'll all have more energy tomorrow for wherever we end up going."

"He's right, Guildersen," Abernathy said, from where he was lying down in the street with an arm over his eyes. "I haven't walked this much in a week, let alone a single day. Even if the rest of you are ready to go, I couldn't get very far. We need a break."

"Fine!" Guildersen bent down, spittle flying out as he spoke directly to Tuya. "We'll stop here, but you will be on your feet and ready to leave as soon as the sky begins to lighten. And you'll go where I tell you to go." He turned away, stopping beside Robbins long enough to scoop up the cans Tuya had dropped, and then walked toward the nearest house.

Tuya watched him, wishing she had a flechette rifle in her hands. With a target that large, she knew she'd never miss.

FIFTEEN

He woke on a soft mattress, under smooth sheets, and threw his arms up to stretch them out. After returning from the *Indomitable*, President Meyers had stayed aboard the Coalition frigate for a few hours. Meeting with the ship's senior staff, he'd sketched out everything discussed with Admiral Yumata and waited for their impressions. Commander Richtaus had remained silent, keeping her own opinions inside until she heard what her captain and admiral had to say. Both men still felt that there could be no compromise with the Syndicate ship, and Yumata's words only convinced them of it.

The ride back to Luna on the *Vagabond* had been interesting, with Captain Frost smiling and happy for the first time in a couple of days. Meyers couldn't decide if the young captain were happy they'd made it off the cruiser, or because there didn't look to be a chance of cooperation. He just wished he could share that joyful feeling, instead of the stone in the pit of his stomach when he thought about how close they were to another battle. He'd lost too many of his people and ships already, and didn't like the thought of losing more.

After dismissing Dex on his return to the Hall, knowing she'd find her way aboard the docked *Vagabond*, Meyers spent a few hours replaying the meeting in his head while watching close footage of the cruiser on a loop. Every word Yumata had spoken could be taken either way, the ultimate example of noncommittal negotiation. Except for the part where he admitted he had overthrown the appointed captain but still hoped to work things out with the ruling committees.

There had been something in the man's eyes when he said those words, a look that made Meyers feel certain it was some kind of ploy.

He finally shut everything down after midnight, deciding he needed to spend a night in his own home for once. Sleeping on the couch in his office saved time, but he was getting too old to suffer the lumpy cushions for more than a few nights. His neck and shoulders were constantly tight with stress, and sleeping on that couch wasn't helping.

It was still early when he crawled out from under the silk sheets, an extravagance he never regretted when he had a chance to enjoy them. The home AI system had woken him with gentle music and a slowly brightening room that simulated sunrise. His shower started spraying water the moment his foot touched the tiles, and coffee was already waiting in the kitchen by the time he'd shaved and dressed. It was enough to give a man an enthusiastic optimism as he started his day.

Meyers walked to his office every day, enjoying the open air feel of the dome and the majestic view of Earth or the stars whenever he looked up. The interior lights were still dim this morning, and he was able to see a great speckled swath of the universe. His secret dream was to build a government that would one day fill the planets around some of those stars, expanding the reach of humanity and helping them become greater than they were. It was a dream that felt a tiny bit closer, now that he was working to build the Colonial Alliance into a real entity.

The Alliance Hall was almost empty when he entered. A handful of people were hard at work already, and he almost asked them if they'd arrived before him or never left. He was proud of the dedication so many of his workers felt, but also wanted them to take care of themselves and not burn out too soon.

His first real surprise of the day was finding a message from Rinde Brighton waiting on his display. Brighton wanted to hold a meeting in Armstrong dome later that morning, along with several of the hastily elected representatives. More than a thousand people had been rescued from the factory, and all but a few fully supported the splinter government that had been formed. Meyers knew it was important to maintain that support, and also to keep them in favor of working with the Alliance. That would make it easier for them to recognize his new government's legitimacy later on. He sent a quick reply, agreeing to the meeting.

His second surprise came when Dex walked through the door only half an hour after he arrived. She was smiling and humming, which made him laugh. "What I wouldn't give to be young and in love again," he said as she settled into the chair behind her desk. "I take it you and Captain Frost had a great evening."

"It was wonderful, sir. The crew gathered in the rec room and we all watched an old movie. *Star Trip* or something like that. It was so funny to see the way people back then imagined the future would look."

Meyers shook his head, thinking that he knew the film she meant. He'd watched it as a kid, feeling that same hilarity at the future on the screen that was so outdated compared to his own present. The only things the people in the movie had that wasn't already surpassed were the warp drive and transporter technology. That was technology that still seemed centuries from reality, if it could ever happen at all.

Physicists were still divided on the feasibility of the proposed options.

"I hate to drag you down after such a wonderful night, but we have a lot of work ahead of us today." He told her about the meeting in Armstrong, which she added into the daily calendar and shifted other things to make room. "I want you to check in on that third fusion reactor that is being built. See if they could fit in another one. I'd like to get as many of our ships upgraded as possible before things go pear shaped."

"You don't think Admiral Yumata will hold to his agreement not to attack?"

"I think he's just buying time to get his own ship ready, as much as I hate to admit it. I'm sure Erik told you all about the meeting, and probably enjoys that nothing got accomplished." He said the words with a slight smile, taking away some of the bitterness.

"Erik would never be happy about your failure, sir, but I do admit he was ecstatic that it appears he doesn't have to worry about the *Indomitable* joining our forces. As you can imagine, he has a strong aversion to such an outcome."

"Captain Fitz would seem to share that, based on their reactions. Speaking of, we need to get Tom in here this morning. I want a progress report on those Armstrong volunteers, and his estimate on when they could be deployed. I also want an update from our sources on Earth. Is the Coalition resistance holding back the Syndicate invasion, or just slowing it?"

Dex turned to her display, and started to work on his requests right away. This was the part of being a leader that most people never considered, the myriad pieces of information he had to absorb and work around each day. For the moment, he felt certain the *Indomitable* wouldn't attack his ships. However, Yumata had also made it clear he wouldn't allow any troops to be sent down to help fight against the Syndicate military. There would come a time when he'd have to decide which was most important for the long term stability of the system, and he was afraid that time was coming faster than he'd like.

Tom arrived a short time later, standing in a relaxed stance with his hands clasped in front of him. Meyers was always amazed at how quickly the military demeanor had descended as soon as he took over the leadership of the Alliance Marines. "We have six squads, ten soldiers each, fully trained and equipped, thanks to Vice President Avila's hard work. Forty three people in Armstrong have volunteered to receive training, and are progressing nicely. We usually have a handful or so new people wander in each day to join them, so that group is growing."

"How do you feel they'd fare if we gave them weapons and dropped them on Earth to help defend Coalition territory?"

Captain Fitz stared into space above his head, calculating his best response. "Used in a purely defensive formation, I believe they'd prove to be adequate, sir. If we asked them to go on the offensive and join an attack, I can only say they'd perform better than untrained civilians."

Meyers was happy with that response. "It's not like we're going to load them on ships today and start taking them down, but it's going to happen at some point. Do your best, captain, and let's hope they have time to greatly improve before we do commit them."

They discussed the status of the supplies available for the military, and decided they had enough armor and weapons for their current Marines. Recruits from the planet were no longer coming in with the inability to get ships past both the *Indomitable* and the Coalition ground fire that now targeted anything in their airspace. They'd been lucky to avoid any damage when the attacks started during the evacuation of the factory.

Dex had a report from their sources on the ground after Captain Fitz left, and it was disheartening. More than half the Coalition military was now fighting back against orders from the corrupt prime minister, but they were overwhelmingly outnumbered by the Syndicate forces. The Executive Committee had pulled all but a few troops from every corner of their territory, committing them to the invasion. They still managed to take several kilometers of ground every day, pushing back the defenders.

Even worse, the death toll among civilians was climbing as the two armies were meeting in heavily populated areas. Despite warnings and commands to vacate their homes, too many people stayed and risked their lives. All too often, it was a risk that did not pay off for them. More than three hundred thousand civilians were confirmed dead since the invasion began, and more than twenty thousand soldiers. The deaths were heavily on the Coalition side of the ledger.

The prime minister was still holding daily speeches, decrying the splinter government on Luna. He called them nothing more than tools for an overambitious, power hungry leader that wanted to take control without benefit of elections. At the same time, he announced that the elections only months away would be postponed in light of the invasion. His country needed stable leadership. A statement that made Meyers laugh bitterly, reflecting that their leadership were the ones that sold them out and allowed the Syndicate to push so far into Coalition territory and take so many lives.

As he grabbed his jacket, slinging it around to slide his arms into the sleeves, his brain was already churning through everything that would need to be discussed with Rinde at the meeting in Armstrong. They had to find a way to build support on Earth, which was proving harder than expected. His contacts in the networks that had allowed their first announcement to be broadcast across the planet now reported government agents in place to vet and approve anything released.

The tunnel that connected Aldrin and Armstrong, buried twenty meters below the lunar surface, had been fully cleared now. Workers still toiled, installing better supports to ensure it couldn't be so easily blocked in case of any future attacks. The checkpoints that used to be occupied by Coalition and Syndicate soldiers were disassembled, allowing for free traffic flow between the domes. Meyers waved at people who called out in recognition, and declined several offers of a ride on motorized carts being used to transport people and goods. If he couldn't make the walk in Luna's light gravity, then his health was in more trouble than he ever expected.

Rinde was waiting at the entrance to Armstrong, his white smile bright in his dark skin. He raised his arms in greeting, wrapping Meyers in a friendly hug. "It is so good to see you again, my friend. I must admit that I had concerns on whether you would ever return from the lion's maw."

He chuckled, patting Brighton's back. "I had young lions of my own along, just in case. I don't think they would've considered doing anything to me, with the threat of the *Waterloo* and our freighters looming."

"Small threat indeed, against such a large ship as that cruiser. I pray every day that we will be able to finish our new frigates in time." The Coalition had authorized construction of two new frigates in the orbital station's shipyard during the early days of the war. Despite funds being set aside, Brighton had learned that few credits and little of the necessary materials had been delivered.

"I'm afraid we won't have that long, or anything near it." Meyers shared his impression of the meeting, and the things he'd seen from the footage taken during their arrival and departure. "That ship is getting more dangerous with every hour, and I'm beginning to think Captain Frost and Admiral Holgerson are right to be concerned about delaying."

"It is not a light decision to make," Brighton said. They began to walk toward the building that had been set up as his home, with the first floor turned into a makeshift Parliament for the dozen elected representatives. "If you are wrong, many lives could be lost. Without our ships, the *Indomitable* would have no impediment to beginning orbital strikes and destroying any chance of turning back the tide."

"Have you heard anything from Earth?" Meyers asked, stopping before they entered the building.

"My sources dwindle," Brighton admitted. "Every day, I hear from fewer of them. Some are being arrested by the prime minister's personal security force, and others are disappearing and never seen again. We must find a way to get this government to Earth, Anton, or our cause will be lost before we can even begin to fight."

It was the news he'd been afraid to hear, confirming the information from his own sources. Brighton had a presence on Earth after two decades in Parliament and then as Minister of Defense, but his name was quickly being forgotten as people feared for their own lives. It was hard to care about political squabbles or give time to examine the situation deeper, when you expected soldiers on your doorstep at any moment. Time was growing short for both of them, and they would have to act soon.

SIXTEEN

Vegley examined the device laying on the admiral's desk, with wires and exposed circuit boards on display. The spy had talked fairly quickly, telling them almost everything. The woman had even explained her motivation, as if that mattered to anyone. She was a traitor to the Syndicate, and that's all that counted. The only thing the spy hadn't revealed was the location her reports were sent to. She claimed not to know, that the machine itself decided, but Vegley didn't believe it for an instant.

Yumata was inspecting the components with her, listening to one of the ship's technicians explain everything they'd found from an examination of it. There wasn't much to tell. "It transmits on a frequency that's very low on the spectrum. It's an older frequency that hasn't been in use for at least fifty years. Very short range, compared to our current communications spectrum, but still good for a hundred thousand kilometers or so before it starts to degrade at an exponential rate."

"So this couldn't be used to communicate with Luna, or the ships in orbit?" That's all Vegley really wanted to know.

The technician hemmed and hawed a bit before admitting that it could. "You'd need a receiver with absolutely no interference between it and the transmitter, but it could work. I'd say the likelihood of that receiver being in the domes is much lower than being on one of the ships in orbit."

"The *Waterloo*," Vegley spat. "It has to be. The spy admitted she was sending messages to the Coalition."

"The much more likely answer is that she was sending to someone on Earth, yes?" Admiral Yumata looked at the technician with his usual expressionless mask.

"Yes, admiral, I'd agree that's much more likely. It would have to be a location in the visible part of the planet, however. Anything over the horizon would get an unreliable portion of the signal."

"Put it back together," the admiral said, waving at the components scattered on his desk. "I will compose a message, and we'll have our spy transmit it this evening at the normal time." The technician saluted, gathering the pieces into the plastic box. He scooped it up and left the office, seemingly relieved to be away from the presence of the two most senior officers on the ship.

"What should we say?" Vegley asked once they were alone. "We could feed them misinformation, tell them that it'll be weeks before the ship is ready for battle."

"Mmm, I am more concerned about who is receiving the information, commander." She glanced at him questioningly. "Has it not occurred to you that this spy could be sending information to our own government?"

"What? Why would anyone do that, when they could have open reports sent at any time?"

Yumata snorted. "You don't know the Intelligence Committee. They seem to think everyone is against them, and will resort to measures such as these to satisfy their own paranoia."

"If you'll give me an hour with the woman, I'll find out who she's working for." Vegley didn't like the thought of what she might have to do, but for something this important she could set aside her personal distaste.

"No, that won't be necessary, commander. No matter who our spy was sharing information with, we know it's getting to President Meyers on Luna. We just need to hold him off for a few more days, until we can get more of our railguns repaired and replaced." He was lost in thought for a minute, and she watched his face patiently. She kept hoping she'd learn to read his expressions, but so far she couldn't even tell if he had any. "We will release a data stream about catastrophic issues with railgun emplacement seventeen. Have the crews there create some kind of fire or sparks this afternoon, in case anyone is watching."

"I'll make sure it gets done, admiral." Vegley had to admit it was a good plan. Letting them think the *Indomitable* was struggling to complete repairs would calm any worries. The only caveat was that it could convince them to make an aggressive move while the cruiser was still perceived as vulnerable. That wouldn't be a bad thing, either.

She saluted and left the office, pausing on the command deck long enough to check in with the officers manning the stations there. Everything was working smoothly again, a gratifying result of having the admiral back on the ship. Guildersen's command had been so erratic that everyone had been too worried about who would be singled out for punishment instead of focusing on their tasks.

On the way to railgun seventeen, she reached out to the head of Construction & Maintenance to make sure a team was waiting for her with the required tools. They would manufacture a light show large enough for any observers on Luna or the *Waterloo* to see. To make it appear as accidental as possible, she would time the event so that it occurred when both were just appearing over the horizon.

It took most of an hour to rig the explosion and shower of sparks that flared out seventeen minutes after Luna appeared over the horizon. She felt it was poetic to have the timing match the number of the gun port. Vegley watched with pleasure as the crew on the hull raced around in pantomime, much as they would in a real emergency situation. Watching from her display nearby, she felt certain that any observers would believe there had just been a catastrophic failure with the weapon. In reality, it was one of the few guns not damaged on the trip to Earth.

Admiral Yumata was waiting at the rail when she returned to the command deck. He turned with one of his rare small smiles as she stepped up beside him. "Excellent work, commander. Anyone watching that display will be convinced of our distress."

"Thank you, sir. When will you have the spy send our message?"

"I'll wait until the early morning hours. Let them wonder for a while. I'm sure their imaginations will provide plenty of wonderful possibilities."

Vegley waited beside him in silence for a while, looking over the bustle on the bridge below. The crew there were in a much better mood than they had been several days before. The last young woman to be selected by Guildersen for one of his sadistic punishments was hard at work. The Marines had released her as soon as Yumata regained control of the ship, and Vegley hoped the woman knew how lucky she had been.

"What are our next steps, sir?" she finally asked quietly, glancing around to make sure no one was near enough to overhear.

"That is still up to the Executive Committee," Yumata said. "I have sent a request for a meeting with them, so that we can discuss the issues I have seen with military leadership during my brief stint on the Military Committee. It is my hope that we can talk it out rationally, and agree to some necessary policy changes."

Vegley hoped that would be possible, as well, but she wondered if the committee would agree. In her experience, telling the people in power that they were doing things wrong was not the sort of thing that went over very well.

SEVENTEEN

Tuya and Altan selected a house one street over from where the other three found beds. She didn't want to be close to them even when everyone was unconscious. They discussed setting a guard, but decided against it with how drained they felt. She tossed and turned for a while, unaccustomed to a mattress that was so soft, but exhaustion finally overtook her.

It was still dark outside the window when her eyes snapped open. She wasn't sure what had woken her, but knew something had disturbed her sleep. Tuya stayed as still and silent as she could, breathing evenly and slowly to appear asleep. Her eyelids were closed to mere slits, letting her look at the small part of the room she could see while on her side.

Her ears felt like they were on swivels, as she strained to pick up any unusual sounds. They were in a place she'd never been before, so everything was beyond the norm for her. She counted out the seconds, reaching ninety without hearing or seeing anything that might have alerted her into wakefulness. She was about to forget it and let herself go back to sleep when she heard the sound of footsteps on gravel. Not too close, but no more than a few houses away.

She thought about the gravel footpath she and Altan had walked down when they approached this home, and the different pitch of the noise based on their steps. She thought this person was more Altan's size than hers. Maybe Abernathy or Robbins, but Guildersen would be making a deeper crunching sound. *Why would either of them be walking around in the middle of the night?*

The sound stopped, and she knew that whoever it was must have stepped onto the dry grass that surrounded the homes. They weren't trying to be stealthy, walking on the gravel for so long. But she wasn't going to take any chances. Tuya rolled off the bed, crouching on the floor and moving over to where Altan was snoring quietly.

She put her hand on his chest, shaking gently until he woke with a snort and mumble. "What?"

"Alt, someone is walking around outside."

"So?" He rubbed a hand across his mouth, wiping away a trail of drool. "Maybe one of the other guys is restless?"

"Possible, but better safe than sorry."

They heard the crunch of gravel again, closer than it had been before. Tuya held up a finger, turning her head to listen. Six rapid footsteps, and then silence again as the person stepped onto grass. "That's next door. They're definitely searching for something."

Altan didn't look convinced, but allowed her to lead him out of the bedroom and along a short hallway into the living area. The windows there had wispy curtains, and Tuya crouched to the side of one and pushed the curtain aside just enough to have a narrow view of the yard outside. It was pitch black with the power shut off in the town.

She kept her eye to the crack, searching for any movement and listening for footsteps. Altan yawned loudly behind her, and she heard a creak as he sat on an old fabric couch. She gritted her teeth, wondering if she had woken him for nothing. Minutes passed and she heard nothing more, so perhaps it really was just one of their companions restlessly roaming the area.

A flash of light drew her attention, coming from the nearest cross street. Then she heard faint voices in another direction. It was hard to pick up the words, but the tones didn't match what she knew of their fellow *Indomitable* cast-offs. She twitched the curtain to get a better view, and froze when a shadow flitted across the window. A figure walked past the front of the house, a man in a dark uniform carrying a rifle. Definitely not one of their companions.

Tuya hissed, then hissed again when Altan didn't look up. He finally jerked his head up, and she was irritated to see that he'd fallen asleep. She waved her hand, beckoning him to get closer. He crawled across the carpeted floor, raising his eyebrows as he got closer. "There are people out there," she whispered. "At least three, probably more."

He didn't look too convinced, opening his mouth to question her information. A light hit the window before he could speak. Tuya slowly dropped the curtain, trying to avoid drawing attention. Then she scooted a few inches away, keeping her back tightly against the wall. Altan dropped to lie flat on the floor. The light moved across the window, illuminating the room through the thin curtain.

The light shut off after a few seconds, and she heard quiet footsteps continue past the house. The night was filled with a steady rumble as an engine started nearby, and two male voices called out all clears. Tuya released the breath she'd been holding, moving slowly to lift the curtain and peer out once more. The light she had seen down the street earlier was brighter now, resolving itself into a headlight as a personnel carrier rolled slowly down the asphalt street. Five soldiers appeared from various points along their street, walking to catch up to it.

"Shit," she whispered. "It's Syndicate soldiers, sweeping the town. Once they find Guildersen, we're in trouble." Tuya released the curtain and pulled back to look at her brother.

Altan was shaking his head slowly. "You were right. We should've left last night."

"Even I couldn't have anticipated this." She looked around the room, hoping to find some kind of makeshift weapon. She'd already looked for kitchen knives in every house, and found only flimsy plastic examples left behind by fleeing homeowners. The legs on a sturdy wooden chair looked promising, but breaking one loose would generate too much noise.

"We need to get back to that small grocery store, grab the bag of food we left there."

"We can't risk it." She flicked the curtain aside, picturing the layout of the town in her head. The store was a few blocks behind the house, the same direction the soldiers and vehicle had been moving. If she were in charge, there would be more personnel carriers combing the town from other directions, as well. "Grab what you can, and then we need to move."

They spent a minute frantically searching cabinets for anything left behind. The pantry was depressingly bare, containing a sack of rotted apples and one dented can of prunes that was at least a few weeks past the expiration date. Tuya wasn't entirely sure of the current date, but Altan seemed to be more confident. Regardless, they grabbed it and stuffed it into a pillowcase with a box of pasta and powdered cheese. There was also a bottle that was half full of vinegar. She had no intention of drinking it, but grabbed it so they could fill it with water later.

Altan picked up a few utensils from the kitchen, a stainless steel spatula and hard plastic potato peeler. She lifted an eyebrow at him, but he shoved them into the bag. "Just in case." He wanted to search the bathroom for anything useful, but she was feeling pressure to be on the move. She grabbed his wrist and pulled him toward the side door that exited onto a covered parking spot. The car that should have been there was gone, as was every other functioning vehicle in the town as far as they could tell from the daylight inspection.

They stayed low as they ran between houses, sticking to the shadows as much as possible. Tuya really wished they could have found a flashlight, even though she knew she wouldn't dare to use it this close to the soldiers. Once they reached the final house on the street, she paused long enough for both of them to catch their breath. She looked down the cross streets, listening attentively for any warning of a vehicle's approach. Satisfied there was nothing, she waved for her brother to follow and sprinted as quickly as she could.

A light came on when they were halfway across the street, followed by a shout as the searchlight was turned to find them. Tuya cursed and sprinted harder, barely staying ahead of the bright light that was trying to pin her down. The shadows of the first house on the next street were only meters away when she heard a grunt and puff of air behind her. She knew immediately what had happened, stopping in her tracks and turning to look back.

Altan lay sprawled on the sidewalk. He had misjudged the height of the curb and tripped. The searchlight swallowed him up, and there were more shouts from the truck far down the street. The engine roared to life, drowning out the running footsteps that had preceded it. He looked up at her with resigned eyes, mouthing for her to run.

Tuya shook her head, clenching her jaw so hard that her teeth felt like they were being driven down into her gums. She knew she couldn't leave him. She'd sworn it to herself, that if she ever found Altan she would never leave him again. No matter the situation or the consequences. She dropped the pillowcase, feeling a numbness spread across her body as she stepped forward.

"No!" Altan screamed. "Run, Tuya! Run!"

She didn't say a word as she walked slowly into the circle of light, kneeling down to take her brother's hand. Seconds later, soldiers swarmed over them. Tuya was thrust into the dewy grass, her face pushed down so hard she was surprised her nose didn't break. Her arms were wrenched behind her back, and metal restraints snapped closed over her forearms. Altan was receiving the same treatment, his neck twisted so he could stare at her with agonizing defeat.

A rifle poked her in the ribs, and strong hands yanked her up by an elbow. Tuya grunted at the pain as she felt something pop in her shoulder. She refused to give the bastards any satisfaction of knowing how badly it hurt. Altan suffered the same rough handling, and she could see he also had a soldier standing behind him with the flechette rifle primed to end his life if he tried something.

"What do we have here?" a woman asked. Tuya turned to see the newcomer silhouetted by the bright light shining from the top of the truck jerking to a stop not far away.

"I saw them, lieutenant!" The voice belonged to a scrawny soldier, and his voice broke on every other word as if he were still going through puberty.

"Good for you," the woman said disinterestedly. "They're wearing detention gear. Did they escape from one of the camps?"

Tuya wasn't sure what she was referring to, but felt she'd vastly prefer they believed she came from whatever camp was referred to than the truth. She opened her mouth, and immediately felt a rifle butt slam into her stomach.

"You speak when the lieutenant asks you to speak," the cracking voice said indignantly.

"Throw them in with the others," the woman said. "We'll sort this mess out when we return to B-91." With that, she turned and walked back toward the light.

Tuya heard the creak of a heavy door opening, followed by the slam of it closing seconds later. The rifle barrel poked her ribs, prodding her to walk forward. Altan jerked as he felt a similar jab, falling into step beside her. He was limping slightly, and she wondered if he had sprained his ankle in the fall. "Why didn't you run?" he whispered, leaning in to be close to her.

"No talking," the scrawny kid said. He shoved between them, glaring at them in turn. Tuya almost laughed to see it, when he was no more than a few inches taller than her short height and carried maybe ten extra kilos. He was not the sort of soldier to strike fear into anyone, and she wondered if that's why he'd ended up on whatever detail this was. Far from the fighting.

They were led to the rear of the personnel carrier, where the doors were open with a narrow ramp laid out. Altan was pushed up the ramp first, with Tuya a step behind. They were halfway up when she ran into his back, and realized he'd stopped in shock at whatever was inside the truck. Leaning over as much as she could without losing her balance, she peered into the dim interior. She snorted when she saw their three companions, all in restraints. Guildersen was unconscious, with a large welt on the side of his head where he'd obviously been hit with something heavy.

Abernathy turned as a soldier entered to push Altan and Tuya into seats, his eyes pleading. "I am a member of the Military Committee. I swear I am. Just look me up in the system. I'll give you money, lots of it."

"You'll be checked out when we return to Camp B-91," the kid said dismissively. Tuya almost chuckled, until she realized that she and her brother were headed to the same place. Not even two days of freedom. She'd hoped it would have lasted a little longer than that.

EIGHTEEN

Erik lifted the glass to his mouth, sipping at the strong liquor that he'd been nursing for most of an hour. His crew was gathered around the table, laughing and joking with one another as the bar grew less crowded around them. Even Mira had left the *Vagabond*, coaxed away from the pilot station by the lure of watching a football exhibition between two teams selected from Aldrin and Armstrong. It had been the idea of Prime Minister Brighton, a way to bring the two different sets of people together and give them a reason to commingle.

After the game, won narrowly by the Earthers currently occupying Armstrong, Erik and his crew had been swept up in the fervor and followed a large mixed group to the nearest bar. Aldrin residents toasted the victors, and Armstrong residents toasted the hard competition. It was good to see the two groups building bonds over something as simple as a game. He had to admit that politicians could come up with a superb idea now and then.

He'd been feeling less and less excited as the night went on, however. His ship had been parked on one of the three functional docking pads attached to Aldrin too much since they returned from taking a fusion reactor out to the *Waterloo*. He was chafing with the desire to be out there, doing something. It had to be much the same with other crews. The freighters had been driven by profits for so many years, always looking for that next job that would put some credits into their pockets. Now the ships were holding a defensive screen around Luna, with the Alliance promising to cover running costs. There had been no talk of pay for the crews yet, and Erik wondered how many people were considering leaving the ships to look for work elsewhere. He knew from experience that life on warships was not something most people were cut out for.

Looking around at his own crew, he had to smile fondly. Built from the remnants of two different ships, they had meshed together well over the months they'd been together. Fynn and Isaac had served aboard the *Vagabond* for fifteen years, old friends that he couldn't imagine being without. He still turned corners on the ship now and then expecting to see John or Sally Murphy, the two who had been lost when Interamnia was destroyed by the *Indomitable*.

Jen had settled in as the ship's doctor easily, and into Isaac's life just as smoothly. The two were holding hands now, and he'd seen them sharing a quiet moment in a dark corner of the room not long ago. It still amazed him that the shy technician had managed to find love in such strange circumstances.

Mira, on the other hand, loved no one as much as she had come to love the ship she piloted. Erik had heard her talking to her display many times, as she tweaked settings or made improvements to programmed maneuvers. He often wondered if she'd crooned to the *Telemachus* in the same way, when she'd served as pilot aboard that ship. He'd asked Jen, but she only smiled and said some people got attached to their jobs more than others.

The five of them made a great crew, but he knew they still needed more hands. He kept thinking about Tuya, who'd been his cargo specialist for years. His heart ached whenever he realized she wasn't there anymore. The *Waterloo* had traced the shuttle from the cruiser that their spy said contained Tuya and her brother, but it had landed behind the invasion forces. As much as he wanted to rush down to Earth and lead a heroic rescue, he knew it wasn't possible in the current circumstances.

Thinking of the *Indomitable* made the taste in his mouth turn sour. The latest data burst had told them about one of the railguns malfunctioning, coming very close to exploding and destroying a large section of the cruiser. He'd used that information to try and push President Meyers into attacking again, but the politician wanted to reach out to Admiral Yumata and see if the setback had softened the man's stance on working together. There had been something in Meyers' eyes, though, that made him think it wouldn't be too long before the leash was removed.

"I'm so wired right now!" Mira shouted, setting off a round of laughter. "Let's go find a place where we can dance."

"It's two in the morning," Jen pointed out. "We should be getting back to the ship for some sleep."

"Sleep is boring. You want to dance!"

Jen looked to Isaac, who surprised them all by smiling and nodding. "Okay, let's go dance."

"I'm going with you," Fynn said, draining the last of his drink. "I have to see this."

Mira slid out of the booth, grabbing the old engineer's hand and pulling him with her. "Keep up with me, old man, and this could be the best night of your life." Fynn looked back at the others with a surprised blush as she pulled him through the door.

"Are you coming?" Jen asked, glancing at Erik.

"No, but you guys go have fun. Burn off some stress, and let those endorphins take over for a while."

"We know where to find you," she said with a wink, pulling Isaac to catch up with the others. Erik watched them leave, and then raised his glass to toast those who were no longer with them before taking a last sip. He swiped his thumb over the pad on the table, authorizing payment of their bill, and then slid out of the booth.

Aldrin was dark and quiet as he left the bar. There was distant music from one of the two clubs that operated almost all night, but that was heavily muted by soundproofing so that nearby residents didn't complain too loudly. He almost expected to hear crickets, even though it had been more than half a lifetime since he'd last heard the insects outside of entertainment programs.

He strolled along the still streets, hands in his pockets and his mind in the stars. During his four years aboard Coalition frigates, he'd increasingly wanted nothing more than a way out of the service. Now, he looked back on those days and wished he had paid more attention to how the ship captains and commanders had comported themselves. If he'd taken in more tactical knowledge, could he have put that to use in the early engagements to end things before the *Indomitable* managed to reach Earth? Or would he have only put his ship and crew into a greater position to face death?

Erik still hadn't come to a conclusion on that as he stopped outside a solid blue door. He placed his palm on the scanner in the middle of it, and with a quiet beep the locks released and he pushed it open. Once inside, he closed the door quietly behind him and then crept up the stairway to the apartment above. A lamp had been left on at the top of the stairs, and he reached out to turn if off once he was on the landing, plunging the room into darkness.

Faint light came through the windows, but it took his eyes half a minute to adjust so that he could see well enough to walk around. The rooms were becoming more familiar, but he wasn't comfortable with his memory of where furniture was and which path he could walk. He managed to make it into the bedroom without stubbing his toe, though he did knock his shin against the corner of a coffee table. Standing beside the bed, he pulled his shirt over his head and then shucked off his pants. Wearing only his boxers, he lifted the sheet and slid under it. He sighed with relief as he settled on the soft bed.

"Mmmm," Dex said, rolling over and throwing an arm around him. "Did you have fun, sweetie?"

"Yeah," he whispered, trying not to drag her too far out of her sleep. "It's good to be back, though." He kissed her forehead, smoothing her curly hair back with his hand.

"Good," she said. Her breathing settled into a steady rhythm as she fell asleep again, and he lay with an arm wrapped around her. Erik was convinced sometimes that the last year had been a dream, never more so than when he realized how much he loved Dex and that she returned the feeling. It was something he'd never imagined happening, even through years of infatuation and awkward attempts at flirting. He decided that he should just enjoy the good in his life, and stop questioning how it happened. With a content sigh, he closed his eyes and drifted into strange dreams.

He woke to the smell of freshly brewed coffee, and found a cup sitting on the table beside the bed. "You're a goddess," he croaked in his sleep-roughened voice as he cradled it and took the first drink.

"And don't forget it," she said from the bathroom, where steam was billowing out after a hot shower. "You'd better get moving if you're going to walk to the Hall with me. Meyers wants us both there by nine for a meeting."

Erik groaned at the thought of more meetings. He wondered if he could sneak aboard his ship and just leave before it happened, and got lost in a fantasy of flying through space with no cares or commitments. It didn't last long, though, as wet curls landed on his face and soft lips met his.

"Move it, mi amor." She poked his ribs, hitting a spot she knew was ticklish and causing him to jump. Laughing, she walked across to the closet to pull out her clothing for the day. He groaned as he got to his feet and headed for the shower.

They walked into the office several minutes before the meeting began, finding President Meyers hunched over the display on his desk. He nodded at them as Dex slipped behind her own desk and Erik took a chair between the two. He didn't have to wait very long.

"Good morning," Meyers said. His eyes were red with dark pouches underneath. Erik wondered if he had slept at all the night before. "The *Waterloo* received another data burst just after midnight, and Admiral Holgerson and I have been discussing how we should handle this. I'd like to get your impressions."

He stood and walked over to the large display on the wall. An image of the *Indomitable* appeared, with several small sections highlighted. "Our spy reports that the defensive guns in these areas are offline, either damaged or destroyed in previous battles. As you can see, this opens up wide holes that we could exploit in an attack. There is even a vulnerability here, around the section the bridge is located in."

Erik stood and got closer to the display, brows furrowed as he examined the image. There was something off about the location of the highlighted areas, but he couldn't figure out why it was bothering him. "What does the *Waterloo* say about this information?"

Meyers pursed his lips before continuing. "Holgerson is uncertain, despite the veracity of previous information. Captain Andrews and Commander Richtaus share his skepticism, and all three feel that any spy who could provide such accurate data should have been sending better information before this."

"It *is* a little strange," Dex said. "It's almost like your visit to the cruiser triggered something."

"It made them realize they had a spy," Erik said, as his brain made connections. He walked up to the display and pointed. "I've spent the last couple of days examining every bit of sensor data the *Waterloo* and our freighters have been able to get, and I'm certain the railguns here, here, and here are repaired and functional. This is even the gun one of the spy's earlier messages told us had been replaced."

Meyers grunted. "Commander Richtaus pointed that out, as well."

"I think whoever is sending us this information is hoping we'll attack those sections. Even if the defensive guns are really nonoperational, our ships would get shredded by the railguns unless we approached from specific angles. And that would open us up to fire from other areas of the ship."

"Admiral Holgerson agrees with your assessment." Meyers sighed and plopped down in his chair again. "You were right, Erik. We should have attacked days ago, not given them the opportunity to make repairs. It's obvious to me that Yumata is doing everything he can to buy time, while also hoping to guide our attacks when it does come to blows."

"I hope this means we aren't going to keep sitting back hoping to persuade them to our side," Erik said.

"I'm meeting with Rinde later this morning," Meyers said. "It is one of the things we are going to discuss. The *Waterloo* takes orders from his provisional government, and without them we don't stand a chance against the cruiser no matter how few guns might be working."

"On the subject of our ships," Dex said, leaning forward to type on her tablet. "Dr. Francks sent down a set of schematics for the weapons improvements they've been working on. Preliminary tests have been promising, and if we can update the systems on the *Vagabond* it should give your heavy railguns at least a fifty percent boost to effectiveness."

"I like the sound of that," Erik said, grinning at the news.

"We also have one fusion reactor completed, and the *Montford* is on pad two already working on the retrofit. A second and third are in progress, and we hope to start installation of those late today or tomorrow."

"Excellent," Meyers said. "I'll let you get back to your ship, Captain Frost, so you can start the process. As soon as a decision is made I'll reach out to you and the other captains."

Erik left the Hall whistling happily. He was hopeful that it wouldn't be too long before they could turn their guns on the *Indomitable*. Friends would be lost in the fight, but it would lead to greater freedom for the system once the Syndicate's last presence off Earth was no more.

NINETEEN

After Rinde was taken by the men in black suits, she had followed her orders from the Prime Minister's office to keep any callers at bay. She would tell them he had just stepped out for a meeting or that he was taking an afternoon off, and promise that he would call back as soon as he could. It took no more than a few days for people to indignantly demand to be put through. All the while, her worries over her own safety continued to grow. The men in black suits had begun to appear around her desk at odd hours, or she'd see them following her on the walk home in the evenings.

One morning, Uju Tyjani woke to find that several items in her apartment had been moved around while she slept. That was the event that finally scared her into leaving, running away before they could decide she was more of a liability than it was worth keeping around. She didn't even pack a bag, just dressed, grabbed her purse, and walked out as if she were on the way to work. Instead of bypassing the subway, she descended and jumped on the first train that arrived. Whenever she arrived at a station with another train across the platform, she would dart across into it just as the doors were closing. After a dozen trips like that, she felt she had shaken any pursuers that might have been following.

She was halfway to the airport before she realized the facial recognition scanners there could be used to track her movements. It was the same at the high speed train station, where security had been upgraded after a few attempted bombings in the early days of the war between Coalition and Syndicate. The only way she knew to get out of the city without being seen was by car, and she didn't own one. It cost more than her annual salary to buy the cheapest model, and she had never lived outside a city with plentiful public transportation options.

A memory of Minister Brighton's friends made her think of a house on the outskirts of town. There had been a reception there half a year earlier, and the man had been excited to show all his guests the five car garage full of classic sports cars. They were never used, except for short trips up and down the estate's long driveway to keep the engines in top shape. If she remembered correctly, the house was vacant much of the year, occupied only when the businessman visited Geneva to influence Parliament members. She felt certain it would be unoccupied now, with the invasion forces three hundred kilometers away and moving fast.

It took most of the day to reach the estate, with the last part of the journey a struggle as she hiked through fields in high heels that were not suited to such terrain. In the end, she pulled them off and walked barefoot through dirt and grass. It reminded her of a childhood spent in a poor village, playing with the other children in their ratty clothes and bare feet.

The house was empty, though she watched it for fifteen minutes to make sure before approaching. As she got closer, she found that many of the windows had been broken and shards of glass covered the surrounding ground. Uju was able to get close enough to look into one of the windows, and found a couple of large stones on the floor of the room. The furniture was knocked over, vases smashed on the expensive carpets. Looters had obviously been through here, stealing whatever they felt could earn them a few credits.

She hoped the cars had been left alone, and hurried around the house to the converted carriage building. Two of the garage doors were open, and her heart fell as she saw the bays were empty. She walked into the first one to find the garage was one large open space. Empty but for one car at the far end. It was a beat up vehicle, and she wondered if the businessman had purchased it for a restoration project.

Uju found a small board hanging on a back wall, with a single keyring on a hook. She grabbed that key, and approached the old car as she said a prayer to her God that it would run. The door squealed as she pulled it open, revealing a leather seat that was cracked and split, looking as if it had gone years without care. Inside, the car smelled of age and dust, with undertones of something she thought might be mouse droppings though she could see none. The sharp edges of the old leather rubbed unpleasantly against the skin of her legs below the short skirt, but she ignored that as she searched for the ignition.

The key turned, the engine coughed a few times, and then the car roared to life. She let out a small shriek of joyful surprise, and looked across the unfamiliar gauges and displays on the analog dash. Uju had no idea what most of the gauges were for, but she recognized the fuel and speedometer indicators. The tank was half full, and she hoped it would be enough to get her far from Geneva.

Learning how to drive the car was the most difficult part. It had been years since her few short lessons, and she'd forgotten much in the intervening years. It was a blessing that the car had an automatic transmission, and she remembered that the P, D, and R settings were the only important ones. She pressed the gas pedal too hard at first, causing the car to jump out of the garage like a racehorse. After a few more jerky starts, she began to get the hang of it.

Until she reached the end of the long drive, and pressed the brake too hard. Her mouth hit the top of the steering wheel, and she felt blood from where a tooth had cut the skin below her lip. She was much more cautious with the pedal after that, and also spent several seconds figuring out how to pull the seatbelt across her chest and click it into place.

She made it twenty kilometers down the road before she realized she had no idea where she was going. When she passed a sign that said she was getting closer to Geneva after she thought she'd been driving away from it, she pulled over at the next fuel station. She was going to fill the tank, but had no idea how or where to access it and didn't want to draw attention to herself this close to the city. Uju pulled her personal tablet from her purse, connected to the mapping application, and looked at routes to get to the coast. She thought she could find a boat there to get across the Mediterranean, perhaps even all the way to Nigeria. Once she was home, she could worry about what to do next.

It was more than three hundred kilometers to the coast by the direct route. She thought about trying to take back roads and avoid any surveillance systems, but wasn't confident enough in her navigational abilities. The trip was smoother now that she was growing accustomed to driving the car, though she heard many honks and angry expletives as other drivers zoomed past her on the expressway. Several times she thought about stopping, driving in the night when there would be far fewer vehicles on the road, but the thought of trying to find her way in darkness was unnerving.

The trip took her longer than it should have, and it was very late in the afternoon when she finally arrived at a port city. Uju praised God for his mercy, getting her this far with so few problems. For the first time since waking, she began to relax and feel as if she would make it home and out of the grasp of the prime minister's minions.

Uju left the car in a public parking lot, slinging her purse over her shoulder and walking down the sloping sidewalk toward the wide expanse of water that she could see over the top of buildings set low on the slope. It was a beautiful sight, and she wished she could have been visiting on a vacation. Near the waterfront, she turned away from the brightly lit tourist destinations and walked instead toward the shabbier warehouses that surround the commercial docks.

The first four ships she checked with refused to even consider taking on a passenger. The captain of the fifth seemed amenable, but balked when she wanted to pay with the loose credit bills in her purse and remain anonymous. However, he did point her toward a rusting old relic at the end of one pier, suggesting that ship might be willing to meet her conditions.

She almost turned around when she got closer to the ship and saw some of the people lounging near the ramp that led into the hold. They were rough looking men and women, the kind she would immediately think of as pirates or smugglers if she saw them in a film. More than a few of them leered at her as she approached, and a wolf whistle caused her to freeze in her steps.

An older man broke off from the small group he had been talking with, turning and walking toward her. His hair and scraggly beard were completely white, and his dark face was crisscrossed with old scars. One such scar traveled across his eye, disappearing underneath a black eyepatch that covered it. His smile was lopsided, with the left half of his face showing little movement. "You're the woman that wants to sneak away, yes?"

Uju stared at him with wide eyes, but he only laughed. "Word travels quickly on the docks, young lady. Quicker than you'd like, I imagine. Where is it you need to go?"

"Africa," she said in a choked voice. "Anywhere in Western Africa."

"Hmm." The captain eyed her, and she felt as if he were undressing her with his eyes. "Our next port is Gibraltar, but I imagine I could find cargo there to get you where you need to go. You will pay, of course."

She nodded, her hand unconsciously patting her purse. "I have credit notes, and will pay you once we have departed." She knew enough not to pay before boarding, risking a dishonest captain leaving her behind and taking the last of her funds.

The captain didn't seem perturbed at all. "Very well, get aboard. We are departing in twenty minutes, and I'll have someone show you to a cabin." He turned away, waving for one of the rough women to walk over. They spoke rapidly in a language she couldn't understand, and after a snort the woman jerked her head for Uju to follow and walked up the ramp into the ship.

Inside, the ship looked to be in much better condition than it had appeared on the surface. The pipes running overhead were shiny and clean, the walls were covered in fresh paint, and the cargo was neatly stacked and tightly strapped in. Uju began to relax at the sight, hoping this ship would prove to be a safe place. The cabin she was ushered into set her further at ease. It was a small, tight space, but the bed linens were clean and the small head was spotless. The rough woman leered and winked before closing the door.

Uju heard a click, and whirled in shock to look at the door. She walked over and turned the shiny handle, feeling it jerk to a stop. The door had been locked, and she could see no way to unlock it from within the cabin. She looked around frantically, hoping to find a key or some kind of sign telling her that the door locked automatically and how to open it. There was nothing, not even a porthole that she could look through and try to get someone's attention.

She banged on the door, hoping the rough woman would be near enough to hear and open it. It crossed her mind that the woman probably locked it intentionally, but she pushed that thought away. Her fists began to hurt from the pounding, and soon she had to stop. There was no way to avoid the thought that she had been locked away on purpose. She shuddered at the thought of why such a thing might have happened, wondering how she would be abused.

The ship shuddered a short time later, and she felt vibration in her feet as the propellers beneath the water began to turn and push the ship away from the dock. She slumped down on the bed, dropping her head into her hands and crying with fear and frustration. She'd come so far, only to end up imprisoned on a ship with no idea of what would happen to her.

It seemed like hours later when the door clicked again, and it opened soundlessly. Uju was lying on the bed, exhausted but afraid to let herself fall asleep. She jerked upright when two men entered the small cabin, crowding the space with their bulk. One was the captain, who considered her with pursed lips. "This is the one, yes?" he asked the man at his side, wearing a black suit and dark glasses.

"It is, captain. The prime minister thanks you for your cooperation with our request. Payment for the reward will be transferred immediately." He then leaned down, close enough that she could see his eyes through the smoky lenses. "Ms. Tyjani, you shouldn't have tried to run away."

Her bed was no more than a row of wooden planks with a blanket laying on top as both mattress and cover. She had six inches of space to either side between the next rows of beds, stacked three high with a ladder at the end for those on the top. The long building, with its canvas walls that were so bad at retaining any cool air, was stuffed with the beds. More than six hundred people lived there, crammed together with no regard to their mental well-being.

Uju had been stuck in the detention camp for almost a week now. She had no idea where the camp was, only that it had taken a long time to arrive after she was removed from the ship. Her head had been covered with an itchy hood, and all she could see through it was flashes of light now and then. Wherever it was, the air was abysmally hot. More so inside the tent, packed with so many warm bodies. She felt as if she would never know coolness again.

Her clothes were soaked with sweat, as they had been for days. She still wore the silk blouse and cotton skirt she had put on the morning she last left her apartment, though she'd long ago shed her heels and lost track of them. No one else in the tent cared if she was barefoot. Some of them had been brought in wearing nothing but underwear, and would still be that way if not for the kindness of others who had an extra layer of clothing to share.

The biggest shock had been the guards. They wore black outfits, so similar to the Syndicate Navy uniforms that she was familiar with. The red rank slashes were on the opposite side of the chest, though, and the red strip was missing along the trouser hems. Either way, these were Syndicate soldiers. Her own prime minister had handed her over to the enemy, ensuring that she wouldn't be found by anyone in the Coalition.

The days were filled with boredom, with nothing for the detainees to do but sit and talk or play handcrafted games. One older man had carved a rough set of dominoes and would play games constantly with others. Uju watched them now and then, but felt so desolate that she couldn't join in.

For an hour each afternoon, everyone in the canvas building was allowed out into the fresh air. They could see nothing but bare dirt and several other similar buildings, but at least she could stand and look up at the clouds and blue sky. Once, she thought she smelled salt on the breeze, but it had been so faint and fleeting she couldn't be sure.

That monotony was broken early one morning, when Uju was woken by the sound of new detainees being pushed into the canvas building. There were three of them, a woman and two men, and they looked as haggard and bedraggled as she felt. Two of them were wearing white clothes that were falling apart, while the other man was wearing a stained and rumpled Syndicate uniform. He drew a lot of glares as the guards pushed the threesome between the row of bunks.

The three beds to the right of Uju's had been vacant for a few days, since the last occupants disappeared through the canvas flap that served as a door and never returned. Now the new people were assigned to those bunks. The man in the black uniform seemed to recognize the hostile glances, and crawled quickly up the ladder to hide on the top bunk. The woman took the bottom bunk while the last man crawled into the middle one. Once they were settled, the guards seemed satisfied and walked away.

Uju glanced across the narrow gap at the new woman, fascinated by the scars running along her arms. She wondered what kind of trauma could have caused such damage. Her gaze drew the woman's attention, and a bitterly disappointed pair of eyes met hers. "I am Uju Tyjani," she said softly.

"Tuya," the woman said. "Sansar. That's my brother, Altan," she said with a jerk of her head to the bunk above. "Where are we?"

"I don't know," Uju replied. "They covered my head when they brought me here, days ago."

"Same for us. The bastards had us in the back of a personnel carrier for most of it, and still made us wear hoods." Tuya turned her head to look at all the other beds around them. It was dim inside the canvas, still dark outside, and it was hard to make out much detail in the gloom. "This is what I get for starting to hope," she said softly, as if to herself.

Uju knew that feeling, all too well. She, too, had started to hope that she was free, only to end up in this place where people were forgotten.

TWENTY

Vegley couldn't keep the frown from her face as she strode through the corridors. Crew and officers she passed cringed back against the wall, hoping not to draw her ire in their direction. She wanted to reassure them that her anger came from a different source, but couldn't bring herself to speak. Her voice would sound even harsher than her face looked.

She bypassed the command deck, stopping near the door that opened directly into Admiral Yumata's office. After pressing her palm against the display, she waited a few seconds before the door slid open. She entered to find the admiral hard at work, and briefly wondered if the man ever slept or took any time away from the rigors of command.

"Commander," he said in greeting, lifting his head to look at her. "What has happened?"

"I got a message from one of my contacts in administration, sir." She grimaced, thinking of the old Academy friend working a desk on the planet and the information he'd passed along. "At zero five hundred hours this morning, five people were picked up by a patrol in an abandoned town eighty kilometers behind the invasion front. One of the men began screaming about being a naval officer, and was wearing the uniform of a captain."

"Ah," Yumata said, leaning back in his chair.

"Yes, sir. They were careful to thoroughly verify his identity, but it was Captain Guildersen. He and Mr. Abernathy were placed on the next available shuttle back to

Hong Kong. The other three have been put into a detainment camp."

"It's interesting that they were all still together, save one. These prisoners were an unexpected complication, and I hope you find out the cause for that request soon, but I would have thought they'd break off as soon as they were on Earth."

Vegley couldn't understand why he was so concerned with the irrelevant prisoners. She'd spent a few hours poring over system logs trying to find out how the transfer order got placed, but hadn't been concerned enough to give it her best effort. In the end, she was quite happy to be rid of them and free up a couple of Marines for other duties.

"Sir," she tried again, "if Captain Guildersen is in Hong Kong, then he is going to be telling the Executive Committee everything about our mutiny. We won't be able to put them off any longer."

Yumata chuckled, rising from his desk to walk around it with his hands clasped behind his back. "I'm sure they've known about it for a day or two now, commander. This is less a complication than a head start. You've taken care of the countermeasures I asked for?"

"Of course, admiral. That was all completed yesterday. We've been giving priority to gun repairs on the belly of the ship, as well, in case of an attempt to board with assault shuttle from Earth."

"They won't come at us directly," Yumata said. "Unless they let Guildersen command the assault, in which case we can bat him away with ease. I fully expect a much more competent leader, however."

Vegley wanted to protest further, but clamped her jaw shut. She knew that she would have to hope the admiral knew what he was doing. From the way he always spoke of an attempt to retake control of the *Indomitable*, it was almost like he'd already lived through it and was looking back on the events. She wondered if tactical masters always looked at situations in that manner.

"What kind of response did our spy's last message receive? Any sign that the *Waterloo* or Alliance ships are trying to sensor map the areas we marked as vulnerable?"

"There have been a few pings from active scanners, but nothing beyond the norm. Two of the freighters did make a landing on the Luna pads earlier today, though that could be coincidence. If I were in charge, I'd want to be doing everything I could to retrofit those junk heaps."

"Possibly," Yumata mused, his eyes going glassy as he looked into the distance. "We may have tried to push our ruse too far. I hesitated about sending such specifics, but the risk was warranted. Keep the Darts flying patrols, but let's give the pilots plenty of rest in case they are needed. Reduce to two fighters at a time."

"Yes, admiral." Vegley typed in a few lines on her tablet, sending the command off to be relayed to the flight group. She knew they'd welcome the chance to make shorter patrols. Once that was done, she scrolled through her own notes to refresh her memory on a few things.

"The crates you brought aboard on the supply shuttle have been transferred." Vegley wanted to ask what was in the crates, but reined in her curiosity. She knew Yumata would tell her when he was ready. In the meantime, there was more than enough work to keep her mind occupied.

"Bay Three has the assault shuttles prepared as you commanded. The five we have left are loaded with the supplies you requested."

"Very good. Pass on my appreciation to the crew for getting that work done so quickly. It is good to see our efficiency is returning to what it was before I left."

"The crew enjoy working for you, sir. Especially after Guildersen, though he could make any other commander look like a shining example of skill." She slid the tablet back into the pouch on her trousers, turning back to the subject that was worrying her the most. "He's going to tell the Executive Committee some kind of fabricated story, you know. Perhaps that I was the one imposing harsh punishments at your command, and that we tried to kill him but a brave pilot took him off the ship."

Yumata sniffed, and she was surprised at the display of amusement. "He very well might, but the man I've had the displeasure of working with for most of the last eight years will be too stupid to realize that some may disapprove of his methods. He will tell them that I poisoned your mind from the start, and that the refusal of everyone to follow his orders had nothing to do with the constant threat of being killed for doing it below his impossible expectations."

He waved at his desk. "I've reviewed the captain's logs during the time of his command, and I'm tempted to release bits of them to media outlets on Earth. The things he did were abysmal enough, but the things he talked about wanting to do were much worse. I sent them in their entirety to the chairwoman of the Military Committee. Mostly to assuage the guilt I feel over betraying her trust in me."

Vegley was very surprised to hear that admission. She'd always imagined Yumata as someone with little emotion, and yet the way he spoke of the woman he'd worked beside for a short time told of an emotional connection. She wondered briefly if there had been some sort of fling between the two.

"We shall send one more report through our spy tonight," Yumata said as he returned to the chair behind his desk. "Less detailed this time, more of a suggestion of weakness along our starboard flank. Make sure the message cuts out abruptly before it completes. If they think the spy has been discovered, perhaps they will give more credence to the reports."

"Yes, admiral." Vegley had to admire the forethought the command displayed. The railguns on the rear starboard flank had been the ones most damaged when three of the Guild freighters dropped a cloud of debris in front of the Syndicate fleet. The damage from that trickery had been almost catastrophic, rendering them unable to stay and fight the Coalition frigates. It had also been the section that Yumata focused much of the repair work of the last few days on. They had three functional guns on that quadrant of the ship now, enough to do significant damage. "What do we do with the spy once the message is sent?"

"I'm not going to lose a shuttle to send her back to Earth. Put her back in her quarters, under restricted entry. We'll decide what to do once this is over and we know how things stand."

Vegley nodded, then turned to leave the office. She was smiling, a stark contrast to the way she entered. The admiral hadn't said the words, but she could tell that they were close to implementing whatever plans he had been formulating.

TWENTY ONE

Meyers was walking back to Aldrin after a long session with Rinde Brighton and his elected representatives when Dex found him. She was half jogging through the transit tunnel, puffing with the exertion even in Luna's light gravity. "Mr. President, we just received another data burst from the *Indomitable*."

"Oh? Was it as detailed and suspect as the last?"

"No, sir. This stream was as vague as usual, filled with data that suggested a weak spot in the cruiser's starboard rear flank. However, it cut off abruptly. Admiral Holgerson fears that the spy may have been captured."

He cursed, coming to a stop as the ground was beginning to slope up toward the entry into Aldrin. "If that's the case, those Syndicate Marines will interrogate and torture our person until they find out everything that's been shared."

"That was the admiral's opinion, as well. He suggested that we might want to act on the information we have before Admiral Yumata has time to patch the holes in their defenses."

Meyers shook his head in confusion. "We were all mostly convinced the last message was some sort of disinformation ploy. Why would we suddenly reverse that just because this latest message was cut off? It could have just been interference in the signal at the wrong time."

Dex shrugged. "I'm just passing on what Admiral Holgerson said. The *Waterloo* has not wavered in their opinion that we need to push an attack on the cruiser while we have some sort of advantage. Now that the frigate's weapons have been upgraded, they feel it is more urgent."

They continued walking, nearly alone as they entered Aldrin's streets. It was late enough that most people were in their homes or gathered in bars and restaurants. The quiet allowed him to think through everything and try to find any clues he might have missed the last hundred times he ran through it. Unfortunately, there was nothing new that jumped out at him.

"I suppose Captain Frost is on board with the plan to attack, as well?"

"Erik would love to be off the leash," Dex said with a fond smile. "He'll never forget that the *Indomitable* is responsible for the deaths of many people he knew and cared about."

"Arrange a conference for this morning," Meyers said finally. "I want Captain Frost there, along with the *Waterloo* command staff, and Prime Minister Brighton. If we're really going to go on the offensive, then I need it to be a unanimous decision from all parties involved."

"Should I invite the other Alliance captains?"

"Yes, they deserve to know. I only want Frost speaking, though, as the flagship captain."

She hurried off to start sending the messages to arrange things, and Meyers sighed with resignation at going back to his office instead of going home as planned. He wanted to ensure that he was fully prepared for the meeting, ready to lay out the pros and cons for the action they would be considering. A small part of him also hoped that Admiral Yumata would reach out and say that the *Indomitable* was ready to work alongside the Alliance and splinter Coalition government, negating the need for action that could lead to many deaths.

Rinde Brighton arrived at the Alliance Hall early, walking into the office and stopping to cluck his tongue over the way Meyers looked. After a night spent reading and rereading documents, he was disheveled and wan with exhaustion. His jacket had been tossed on the couch hours before, when he gave up on the idea of getting a nap.

"My friend, you are pushing yourself too hard." Brighton took a chair across the desk, crossing his legs and wrapping both hands around a knee. "The stress is not good for a man of our advanced years."

"I only have the one setting," Meyers said with a slight smile. He perked up as Dex entered, carrying a tray with steaming coffee and a large plate of hydroponic fruits and vat grown bacon. "You are a godsend, as always."

Brighton shared the coffee, and they talked as he ate. Meyers filled the prime minister in on everything he'd been checking on during the night, a depressingly small amount of new information gleaned from the massive amount of data that had been accumulated. As he wiped his mouth and drained the last of the coffee, Dex was back to let him know the other participants were all ready and waiting.

The large wall display filled with boxes, small ones showing the faces of captains on the Alliance freighters and two large ones showing Captain Frost on the *Vagabond* and the senior command staff on the *Waterloo*. "Thank you all for joining so early in the morning," Meyers said to start the conference. "As some of you may know, we received a data burst shortly after midnight, purportedly from our spy on the *Indomitable*. Admiral Holgerson?"

The Fleet Admiral, formerly head of the entire Coalition fleet and now only in charge of the last remaining frigate, laid out the details of the message. He also went over the information in the previous message, for those who had not been privy to it until that moment. Meyers watched the faces of his captains, judging their reactions to the information presented. Most seemed skeptical, much as he imagined he would be upon finding out about some spy that no one had known was implanted on the enemy ship.

"Thank you, admiral," he said, taking over again. "The question before us now is do we act on this information and stage an attack on the cruiser, or do we maintain our defensive posture?"

"We have to attack," Captain Frost said, leaning in as he spoke. It made Meyers feel the urgency of his words, apart from the passion in his voice. "That ship has shown many times that they care little for the lives of innocents. We need to take them out while there's still time, before they're back to full strength." Several other Alliance captains nodded, though more than a few looked hesitant. These were men and women who never expected to be in any battle situation, aside from the possibility of running from pirates trying to steal their cargo.

"I agree with that assessment," Admiral Holgerson said. "Even if the information we have received is faulty or bogus, we have scans showing a dozen nonfunctional railguns on the ship. We can target the other emplacements, dedicating our attack to disabling those weapons quickly and efficiently.

That grows much more difficult with each new gun they repair and bring online."

Meyers turned to Brighton, silent until that moment as he listened to the others speak. "Prime Minister, what are your thoughts? The *Waterloo* is under your command, and without her the Alliance ships would stand little chance of success."

Rinde looked grave and thoughtful. "I was in favor of the diplomatic approach from the beginning," he said. "If we could resolve this situation with less bloodshed, then we had to try it. However, every hour that we delay and hope for signs of cooperation, thousands are dying or being left homeless on Earth because we can't assist with the battles there. The time has come for weapons instead of words."

"We are agreed, then." Meyers felt the weight of the moment, and took a deep breath as he paused to let it sink in for everyone. "Admiral Holgerson, would you work with Captain Frost to formulate a strategy for the combined fleet to follow? Present that plan to myself and Prime Minister Brighton at noon, and we will decide on a timeline for next steps then."

The admiral looked pleased as the conference ended, as did Captain Frost. Several freighter captains looked a little queasy, and Meyers made a note to have Dex contact them and make sure they were on board with the plan. If not, those ships would be held back to contribute fire from a distance.

Once the wall display was dark, Brighton stood and buttoned his jacket. His lips were pursed, and Meyers waited patiently until the man was ready to speak whatever was on his mind. "My friend, I have received some news from one of the few people on Earth still in contact with me. He has identified several detainment camps across occupied Coalition territory, where our citizens are being caged and kept out of the way."

Meyers shared the obvious distaste at the idea. "I'm sorry to hear that, Rinde. People shouldn't be treated so poorly, and I can't believe that man who still calls himself prime minister remains intent on working with those who would do such things."

"Yes, it is yet another in a long list of abuses he will answer for. But that is not the information I have for you. My contact has managed to get inside one of these camps, and taken video of the people suffering there. They are disgracefully underfed and most wander around in little clothing." Brighton's jaw bunched up as he fought against emotion. "Most importantly, I have recognized many faces from that video. One is my former assistant, the woman who shared my every move with the prime minister's lackeys. Another..."

Meyers leaned forward, not sure if he was going to like what was about to be said. "Yes?"

"Another was Tuya Sansar, the woman who used to work on the *Vagabond*. I've seen her files, while reviewing everything that happened. She is definitely in the detainment camp near the Mediterranean coast."

"Ah." Meyers leaned back, rubbing a hand over his brow. "If Captain Frost knew that, I'm not sure what he would do. He already wanted to go down and try to find that shuttle when we learned Ms. Sansar was aboard. It took everything I had to convince him not to risk it, but if he has her exact location now I'm not sure I'd succeed."

"You can't tell him," a quiet voice said, and he turned toward Dex, still sitting at her desk. "You can't, sir. He'll risk anything to save one of his crew, and it's too dangerous for him to do that right now. We need him here."

"I can't lie to the man I'm expecting to lead my fleet," he said.

"You don't have to," Dex said firmly. "Just don't mention it. Wait until the battle with the *Indomitable* is over, and then tell him. If our ships survive the encounter, that's when we'll need to start landing troops and helping push back the Syndicate invasion force. He can work on saving her then. Right now, it's too big of a distraction."

Brighton nodded hesitantly. "She is correct, my friend. I wish to save my assistant just as much as your Captain Frost will want to save his friend, but I know we can do nothing at this moment. I must hope that she survives long enough to be rescued. It is a burden on my mind that I would not wish on anyone, and a ship captain about to go into battle should not be distracted with it."

"I'm outvoted," Meyers said. "Fine, we'll keep it between us for now. But I want you to tell him as soon as this is over, Dex. He'll take it better coming from you than me." She nodded, looking unhappy but satisfied.

TWENTY TWO

An hour after they'd been shown to uncomfortably hard beds in the overcrowded canvas building, guards showed up with a trolley piled high with boxes. Each person was given a wrapped bar, about half the size of a normal protein bar that Tuya would have eaten on the *Vagabond* when she was too busy to take a long meal break. She looked at the trolley hoping for water, as well, but there was nothing.

"There are two sinks," the attractive dark skinned woman on the bed beside hers said when she asked. "A metal cup is chained to the faucet, and you must wait in line to get a drink."

Tuya shuddered at the thought of sharing a cup with hundreds of others, especially when she looked around in the growing light to see so many who looked ill. Then she thought about waiting in line to get a drink, and realized that by the time she made it to the water she would be too thirsty to care. "Can you show us where to go?"

The woman, Uju, nodded and led them to the nearest sink. Several dozen people were already waiting as they joined the queue. Tuya watched as the man drinking from the cup coughed up a wad of phlegm that he spat into the sink before drinking again. After ten seconds, the person behind him was already nudging him out of the way to take their turn.

"Who makes people live like this?" Altan asked. He sounded horrified by the situation, a feeling that Tuya shared.

"We are inconvenient," Uju said. "The rules of war forbid them from killing civilians, but it doesn't prevent them from showing as little care as they can get away with. We are fed, we have water, and we have beds."

"It almost makes our last prison look like a five star hotel," Tuya said with a snort. She remembered the hatred she'd felt for the brown mush she'd been served in her cell aboard the *Indomitable*, and wondered how long it would be before she'd trade almost anything to have that back. Probably not too long.

"The Coalition must be fighting them," Altan said hopefully. "If they can push the Syndicate military back, then we'll be freed and get away from these sadistic conditions."

"Do not hope too much for that," Uju said. Tuya wanted to ask about that, but they were next in line. She tried washing the cup before drinking, but after a few seconds a nearby guard yelled at her to hurry up. Holding back her disgust, she filled the cup and drank deeply. After a night with no food or water, she was parched. She started to fill the cup again, and was shoved aside so hard that she fell to the packed dirt floor.

"One cup per person," the guard snarled as he waved Altan forward to take his turn. Her brother cast her an apologetic glance before hurrying forward to get a drink, and she crawled to her feet to brush the dirt from her filthy clothing. She glared at the guard, but he had already turned his attention back to the line as he looked for someone else breaking the rules.

Uju apologized for not explaining the restriction as she rejoined them, but Tuya waved it off. "What were you saying before, about not hoping for the Coalition to save us?"

"The Coalition government put me here," the other woman said, as they walked over to a row of empty crates that had been turned over to make seats. She told them the story of how black-suited men showed up at her door one night, telling her that she would report every word and movement of the man she'd worked beside for almost twenty years. A man she'd come to know as a friend and good person. Uju resisted at first, but then her mother in Nigeria was arrested for murder. The family waited for the police to realize their mistake, but Uju knew what was happening. The moment she agreed to spy on her boss, her mother was released with a half-hearted apology for the error that led to her arrest.

Tuya listened in horror to the arrest of Rinde Brighton, and then in admiration to the journey the woman attempted when she decided to flee. Altan pulled her into a hug when she talked about being locked on the boat and then the black-suited men taking her away with a hood over her head. Tuya couldn't imagine having to deal with that situation after a lifetime of being an office worker. It wasn't the kind of thing you were mentally prepared for unless you faced danger on a regular basis.

She and Altan then shared their stories, going back many years to the start of things for them. It took a long time to tell, but they had nothing better to do. Even when other detainees would wander over to listen to bits of the story, they didn't stop talking until they had told it all. Tuya showed her scars when she talked about the surgery to remove the implants, and the long days of rebuilding her body afterwards.

"You are an impressive woman," Uju told her, staring in fascination at the still pink scars. "I don't think I could have found the strength to go on after something like that happened."

"It's hard to know until you're in the situation. You had the strength to run away when you knew you might face harm. That's more than a lot of people would do."

"No, I was driven by fear. If I had any courage at all, I would have told Rinde everything the moment they forced me to spy on him. I would have helped him to rid our people of corrupt leadership."

"Speaking of corrupt," Altan mumbled, his eyes focused on the flaps on the far side of the building. Tuya and Uju turned to look as a large man in a freshly cleaned uniform entered with half a dozen guards flanking him. He looked around with a smug smile, one that grew wider when he spotted them and waddled over.

"Ah, the Sansars. I trust you will be troubling me no further, now that you're back in a place where you belong."

"Guildersen," Tuya spat out, rising to her feet with her fists clenched. The guards around the officer took a step forward, raising the stun batons they carried. "You better hope I never see your fat face again. I promise I won't be as nice."

He only laughed, a gurgling sound that grated on her nerves. "Threats like that will have you back on my ship, if you're not careful. You won't face such wonderful treatment there, I assure you."

"You mean the ship where everyone was only too happy to kick you off?" She couldn't resist baiting him, smirking as she said it. But he only shook his head, as if disappointed at the attempt. With a wave, two of the guards stepped forward and jabbed batons forward to send electrical current through her body. Tuya felt her muscles spasm painfully as she fell to the ground on limp legs. Altan cried out indignantly, and was jabbed with another baton as he tried to go to her rescue.

"Something to remember me by," Guildersen said, staring at her almost lasciviously. She realized with disgust that seeing her in pain was getting him off. He licked his lips, and then looked away. "Perhaps Yumata will end up here with you, once I've taken the *Indomitable* again. It won't be long. The preparations are already underway."

He laughed and motioned for another guard to prod her with a baton, sending her body into twitching spasms again. The voltage was high enough to cause painful contractions, but low enough to prevent stunning her into unconsciousness. A setting that was against every rule in the book.

"I really have enjoyed our time together, Sansars." Guildersen licked his lips again, and Tuya was repulsed to see a bulge in his trousers. "Perhaps I will have you brought up to my ship, so we can have a little reunion." His gurgling laughter drifted back to them as he waddled out of the building.

Uju helped Tuya back onto a crate, where Altan was already sitting doubled over as he tried to catch his breath. Tuya knew how he felt, as her body continued to have minor spasms that drove the breath from her lungs until she was gasping in air feeling lightheaded.

"That was the man you traveled with the last few days?" Uju asked. "I don't think I would have stayed with someone like that."

"It was more a grouping of convenience," Altan said through gritted teeth.

"One that I'm really regretting," Tuya gasped out. She looked toward their beds, seeing Robbins peering down from the top bunk. "They weren't all bad, just useless in one way or another."

"I am sorry to say it, but if you had left them behind you might not be here with me now." Uju rested a hand on Tuya's back.

"It won't end here," Tuya said, forcing herself to sit up straight. "It can't. We've been through too much, pushed too hard to get through all the obstacles in our way. Something has to happen to save us."

"Maybe," Altan said, leaning back against the canvas wall with his eyes closed. "I'm not finding much reason to be very optimistic right now."

More than anything, that statement sent chills through Tuya. She'd been feeling pessimistic since the moment they saw soldiers sweeping the town they'd been spending a night in, but hearing that her own brother couldn't find any positive thoughts in their situation was enough to send her spiraling down.

TWENTY THREE

"Commander, I'm picking up some anomalies." Vegley turned away from the rail, and strode across the command deck to lean over the sensor station. The lieutenant there pointed at one of her screens, where some contacts were being reported. As they watched, the screen cleared for a few seconds before the contacts showed up again. Closer.

Vegley turned to the communications station. "Get a report from our Dart pilots. Are they seeing anything in quadrant three?"

She waited for what seemed to be hours as the ensign talked quietly with the fighter pilots. A quick glance back at the sensor station showed the contacts getting uncomfortably close to the cruiser when they appeared on the display again. The communications ensign finally turned with a report. "The Dart pilots reports stars are blinking out in that direction, commander. Almost as if something is moving through space between them and those stars, but they can't see anything."

Vegley cursed, pulling out her tablet and tapping the buttons to send a priority alert to the admiral's office. She didn't wait for him to appear before giving orders. "All stations on alert. Have the gun crews report and standby for further orders. Load torpedoes."

The commands were being sent out and the stations coordinated when Yumata entered the command deck. He crossed to the sensor station calmly, bending to watch the screen as the contacts appeared and disappeared a couple of times. "I believe you are correct, commander. Someone is attempting to attack us."

"There's no way it's the frigate or freighters," Vegley said. "We still have them on the scans, around Luna."

Yumata had stepped over to another station, reviewing video taken from the nose camera of a Dart fighter. "These are smaller vessels. Based on what I'm seeing here, I'd say something like our assault shuttles." He watched the video for a while longer, and she saw a slight smile on his lips. "It would appear that Guildersen was put in charge of the attempt to retake the ship, after all."

"Sir?" She bent over to watch the video with him, confused at his leap. If the blinking stars truly were ships coming toward them, they appeared to be approaching from the inner system.

"It's not quite a direct assault, but all they did was launch from beyond the horizon and loop out to approach from another direction. Guildersen, but with someone feeding him suggestions." Yumata turned away, walking to stand at the rail and looking at the large displays showing the edge of Earth's horizon and the stars beyond. "Launch our fighters, commander."

"Yes, sir." She waved for the order to be passed on, and then joined him at the rail. "Should we fire, admiral? They're just inside the range of our railguns."

"No," Yumata said. "I won't give away any information to our friends around Luna. Let us see what our fighters can do."

They stood in silence, feeling the ship turn beneath their feet as the bow was pointed toward the incoming contacts. Vegley saw the half squadron of fighters launch, wishing momentarily that more of the Darts could have been recovered after they were used against the Coalition fleet in the first battle. She thought of the dozens of pilots left behind, in ships that didn't have drives capable of reaching Earth in the few days before the air in the tanks was expended. It was not a pleasant way to go.

The first shots were fired, small caliber weapons mounted on the wings and belly of the fighters. She kept hoping to see a flash of light that signaled a hit on the approaching attackers, but either there were no hits or the hull plating was too thick. Yumata made appreciative noises as the squadron leader split the group and circled the approximate area they thought the approaching ships occupied. The sensors on each Dart were sweeping the immediate surroundings with high frequency lasers, until eventually the displays showed approximate shapes of the ten undetectable vessels.

"Assault shuttles," Vegley said. They looked wrong to her, too angular and flat along the sides; the shuttles currently being prepped in their own docking bay were more rounded and sleek looking. She wondered if that different design somehow explained how the sensors could lose track of the ships.

Yumata looked as if he knew exactly what they were, however. "That is the design Lieutenant Davis and I came up with for Ghost Squad. The stealth properties are something we discussed, but our execution was never this good."

Vegley grunted as she absorbed the information. She'd heard stories about Ghost Squad, the elite group that Yumata had envisioned becoming the new standard for assault and infiltration missions. She'd even managed to catch a glimpse of the soldiers once, wearing their alien-looking suits that seemed to flow over their bodies like a second skin. It had been a shock when the *Waterloo* returned and they learned that the mission to take or destroy the ship had failed.

The admiral turned away, giving a command for someone to report to him on the bridge while she was lost in memory. It took no more than a minute for the doors to slide open, and a man in a Marine uniform entered. He snapped his heels together and raised his hand in a sharp salute.

"Sergeant Anders," Yumata said in greeting, waving the soldier to a relaxed posture. "This man is the sole surviving member of Ghost Squad, commander. He has been working on a few things for me these last few days. Is everything in place, sergeant?"

"Yes, sir," the man said, his voice deep and gravelly. Vegley wondered if it had gotten that way from barking at soldiers as he worked to train them. "Squads five and eleven have performed admirably in our exercises, and I have them ready to meet any invasion attempts. Squad nine has been issued heavy weaponry, and is ready to help repel boarders."

Their attention was drawn back to the large screens as people on the bridge below let out shocked noises. Vegley turned just in time to see the last light from an explosion. One of their fighters had struck an assault shuttle, exploding on contact. The shuttle itself had survived, though the collision had worn away whatever plating prevented them seeing it. Most of the shuttle was now visible, skewing away from the *Indomitable* on another path.

Anders coughed behind them. "Admiral, request permission to lead teams into the fight."

"Denied, sergeant." Yumata pointed to an empty station. "Coordinate from here, and keep me updated."

Vegley was interested to see the disappointment on the soldier's face, and realized he really had been looking forward to putting himself into danger. She wondered if that were a sign of an unhealthy death wish or zeal to do his job and keep the cruiser safe. The thought didn't hold her attention long, as warnings began to blare from multiple stations below.

"Contacts are half a kilometer out," someone called from behind her. "Before they entered the sensor shadow, the group seemed to be splitting. Bay Two and Cargo Hold Five are the approximate destinations."

"Sending my squads to those locations," Anders said. Yumata passed on orders for other Marine squads to attach themselves to the three being coordinated by the sergeant, increasing the firepower of each group.

Vegley and Yumata retreated from the rail, standing near the bank of consoles so they could watch the action on camera views through the ship. She could see dozens of armed Marines staging outside of the indicated locations, all of them carrying flechette rifles instead of stun pistols. It took her by surprise, but she knew she should have expected it. If the Syndicate leadership were sending an attack force, then there would be no accommodation made with the mutineers.

"We have visual," one of the officers said, drawing Vegley's attention to the display that showed a handful of shuttles sliding through the ion barrier of Bay Two. The same docking bay where she'd met Yumata's shuttle not too many days earlier. The crew had already been vacated from the area, and she watched in tense anticipation as the shuttles settled to the deck. The doors on the rear of each dropped quickly and silently, and armored Marines jogged down the ramps. The soldiers raised their weapons to search the bay for any defenders, forming organized ranks as they did so.

"There have to be almost a hundred of them," Vegley whispered to herself.

"At least two squads per shuttle," Anders said, having heard the remark. His voice was filled with professional admiration. "Well trained, too. Look at how quickly they form their squads."

On another display, they saw sparks as a powerful torch sliced through the inner hull of Cargo Hold Five. Vegley knew it would take several minutes for the invaders to cut their way through, and they could never make the hole large enough for a shuttle. She wondered if that might not be the true sneak attack, with the ships in Bay Two designed to draw and hold attention.

"Sergeant, you may deploy our first countermeasure."

"Yes, admiral."

Vegley watched in fascination as the shimmering ion barrier in Bay Two flickered out of existence. There was no sound with the video, but she could imagine the yells of surprise as the bay decompressed and the black armored figures started to get sucked out into space. Most of the Marines acted quickly, engaging their magnetic boots to lock them in place on the deck, but at least twenty of them disappeared through the wide mouth.

The remaining soldiers began to walk toward the exit, taking deliberate steps and insuring that at least one foot was firmly planted at all times. She wondered if they'd increased the odds enough when Anders tapped a few keys and the ion barrier reappeared. At the same moment, the door of the bay control room one level above the main deck opened and Squad Nine appeared. Each pair of Marines was carrying a large gun, which they propped on the railing and attached with magnetic hooks.

Anders spoke a word into his headset, and the guns started to fire on the invading soldiers. The large bullets ripped into them, scarring the deck and splattering it with blood and viscera. Vegley realized she was holding her breath as first one weapon and then another stopped firing and the Marines had to reload. Half of the soldiers below had been chewed up by the attack, but those still alive were crouched and firing at Squad Nine.

"Pull them back," Yumata said calmly. Moments later the Marines detached the magnetic hooks and disappeared back into the control center, carrying their heavy weapons with them.

The main doors of the bay slid open at the same moment, and three squads of Marines ran through to fire on the invading troops. They were caught by surprise, with their attention still turned on the attackers above, and almost a dozen were mowed down before they began to return fire. The fight was brutal and frantic, but brief. Ten minutes after landing in the shuttles, the invading soldiers were completely wiped out. The *Indomitable* Marines had suffered only a handful of casualties.

The shuttle pilots were still on board, and the ships began to lift from the deck to exit the ship. Anders gave a quick order, and several Marines ran forward to fire large guns. Electricity played across the shuttles, as the electromagnetic pulse weapons fried circuitry and killed power to the engines. Vegley grinned as the shuttles dropped back to the deck, and their Marines boarded to take the pilots prisoner.

Yumata was already watching the display that showed soldiers entering Cargo Hold Five. The hole was large enough for two to enter at a time, and they were sweeping the area to make sure defenders weren't hidden behind the crates and pods that filled the chamber. "How long?" the admiral asked.

"Squad Nine is on the way, and should arrive in two minutes."

Vegley wondered how the heavy weapons would work. There was no second level to attack from in the hold. She didn't have to wait long, as Anders gave orders for the four squads outside the hold to enter and attack. Her fist was clenched so hard that she could feel her nails digging into her palm as the Marines ran in and began firing on the invaders. As soon as the heavy weapons squad arrived, they fired from outside the door to devastating effect.

The enemy soldiers were more prepared here, and returned fire seconds after the doors opened. They also had plenty of places for cover, and ducked down behind containers after firing off a few shots. The *Indomitable* Marines concentrated fire on the opening cut through the hull, killing soldiers as they tried to enter through the small ion barrier that had sprung up as soon as the ship detected a hull breach.

Anders chuckled to himself a moment before he tapped in the commands that killed that ion barrier. The hold became a scene of chaos, as the cargo containers were pulled toward the rip in the hole that air was rapidly trying to escape through. Many of the enemy soldiers were sucked out, while their own Marines had already engaged their mag boots as soon as they entered the hold. By the time Anders reinstated the ion barrier, cargo containers filled with tons of material covered the hole and few of the invaders were still standing. It was a quick process to take down the survivors.

Meanwhile, the Darts were making attack runs on the assault shuttles that were maintaining position just outside Cargo Hold Five. The shuttles had no weapons, designed for lightning troop drops or stealth assaults, and the half squadron of fighters attacked them without fear. Vegley watched as one and then another finally succumbed to the heavy fire, until the others turned away and flared their thrusters to get away from the cruiser.

The Darts stayed with them, painting the shuttles with lasers to assist targeting once they entered range of the cruiser's railguns. Vegley waited for Yumata to give the order to fire, but his face was serenely calm as he watched them escape. "Now we all know where we stand," he said. He thanked Sergeant Anders, releasing the soldier to go check on the Marine squads. An order was passed for crews to return to Bay Two and start working on repairs to the newly acquired stealth shuttles.

As they returned to the rail of the command deck to watch the remaining assault ships flee back to Earth, Yumata nodded as if coming to a decision. "The committees will not negotiate, commander. And now they know that we are more than ready to defend the *Indomitable*. It is a stalemate."

"I've never been a fan of those, sir."

"Neither have I."

TWENTY FOUR

Erik watched the replay of the action that Luna's monitoring systems had captured, trying to figure out what caused the six fighters to be sent out. They swarmed around empty space, as far as he could see, firing at seemingly nothing. "Training exercise?"

"I don't know, cap. You'd think they would fire at each other if that was the case."

He and Mira were equally confused, as Tom had been when he contacted them and asked them to look over the feeds. The consensus on Luna was that the *Indomitable* had just experienced a boarding attempt from the ground, perhaps with an approach that was blocked from their view. But Erik noticed the fighters concentrating fire on an area that was well within sight lines. He magnified the screen as much as he could, but even with the best quality equipment the picture started to grow fuzzy and pixelated before he could make anything out.

"Whatever it was," he said when he was talking to Dex over a video link a short time later, "it makes me even more certain that we need to attack. As much as I don't like this Admiral Yumata, I don't want the Syndicate regaining control of the cruiser and turning it on us."

"President Meyers agrees with you," Dex said with a grim look. "His reservations are fading quickly, and Prime Minister Brighton is drafting legislation with his group of representatives to give the *Waterloo* authorization to proceed."

"That's good news, but it's taking too long. What about the reactor installs for our ships?"

"*Montford* is operational and cleared to depart in the next half hour. *Viking* and *Tamerlane* are on pads, and work has started to remove the old reactors. Both ships should be ready within six hours."

Erik bit his lip, not liking how tight that timeline was. Even if they delayed the attack long enough for the upgrades to be completed, they couldn't delay it longer to let the ships do any testing. They'd lost too much time already, and he could feel the opportunity slipping away faster and faster. "I'll make sure Isaac and Fynn work with the crews to let them know what to expect once the fusion reactor is in. It's not perfect, but they can still contribute to the fight."

"You just make sure you take care of yourself," Dex said, narrowing her eyes. "I've been telling my mother wonderful things about you, and if I can't take you to Mexico to meet her when this is all over she's going to think I made you up."

He laughed, feeling some of the tension drain away with his amusement. "I promise that I won't let your mom think I'm a figment of your imagination."

"I'll even make sure he dresses nice and everything," Mira added loudly.

"He better," Dex said with a wink.

After the conversation, Erik unstrapped and floated through the door of the control center. They were in stationary orbit around Luna so they could keep all their sensors trained on Earth and the *Indomitable*. Without any thrust, there was no gravity in the ship. It was something they were all growing more accustomed to, though none of them were ecstatic about it.

He pulled himself down the hall and into the technical room, where he found Isaac floating amid a jumble of wires. Jen was strapped into one of the chairs, tapping buttons on the screen whenever Isaac asked her to. He kept waiting to see a request for them to share a cabin; Mira had told him that Jen hadn't been to her own cabin more than once in the last couple of weeks.

"How's it going?" Erik asked, wrapping his arm through a strap hanging just inside the door.

Isaac didn't even look away from the wires he was twisting together. "The weapon upgrades the *Waterloo* sent over have been input into the system. Every test we've run has completed successfully, so short of an actual test fire I think we're as sure as we can be that it will all work."

"If it's done, what's all this?"

"Isaac had some ideas he wanted to test out," Jen said, smiling fondly as she looked at the bearded tech. "Something about a supernova."

"That's just what I'm calling it," Isaac said. "I had the idea in the shower this morning. If we can charge a torpedo warhead with a massive amount of energy, containing it until impact, we could create an explosion large enough to look kind of like a supernova."

Erik raised an eyebrow. "And you're working on that here? We don't have torpedoes, much less torpedo tubes."

"I'm just trying to cobble together a device that could control the energy retention and release. If I get it to work, maybe the *Waterloo* can do something with it."

Shaking his head in wonder, Erik left them to the work. He knew he'd have to coordinate with Fynn to set up a conference so they could work with the crews on the other ships receiving upgrades to the new reactor technology. Once Isaac started on a "shower thought" project, he had a habit of losing track of time or anything else going on around him.

On one hand, he'd be happy if the supernova warhead could be a feasible technology. On the other, he wasn't entirely sure how much they should share with the frigate. They were working together right now, but with the Alliance asserting control on all territory off Earth, he could see a day when they might be in conflict with the Coalition. He didn't want to face Isaac's ideas being used against them.

He paused outside the reactor room, listening to the voices coming from the engine room beyond. Amelia Houghton, the engineer from Berlin who worked on the final stages of the reactor technology and then came aboard to help install and test it, was still in residence on his ship. She claimed that her conscience wouldn't let her leave until she was positive the reactor was working as expected, but Erik had noticed that she and Fynn seemed to be spending more and more time together. He wondered when he might be seeing a request for a new permanent crew member to join them, and maybe another request for a shared cabin.

Chuckling, he pushed himself back into the corridor to return to the control center. Where his pilot was having a love affair with the ship itself. The *Vagabond* had become some kind of love boat around him, while he was building his own relationship with Dex on Luna.

Two hours later, the orders came through to authorize offensive action against the cruiser. Erik had spent more than an hour that morning speaking with Admiral Holgerson and Captain Andrews, deciding on tactics and dispositions when the time came. He was ready to go, and knew the *Waterloo* was just as eager. Meyers and Brighton agreed on a time to launch the attack, giving them just enough to complete the reactor upgrades on the two ships docked at Aldrin.

The *Waterloo* would be at the center, forming the spine of their attack with her heavy railguns and torpedoes. Three Alliance ships on one side, with the *Vagabond* on the tip of the wing. Four freighters on the other side with the *Montford* on the end. Both had heavy railguns, while the other freighters only had the light railguns the Coalition had given them after retrofitting two of their frigates. All together, their little fleet would have fifteen railguns. The cruiser they faced would have twenty four if she was fully repaired and rearmed.

His only hope was that they hadn't waited too long. Yumata seemed like a smart man, and he had to know they'd come for him eventually. They could do nothing to help the people on the ground until that ship was taken care of. Guildersen may have been incompetent enough to let them land ships for days to empty the factory, but Yumata wasn't beholden to orders from below to keep him in place if they tried such a thing again.

"Uh, cap?" Mira's voice dragged him out of his thoughts.

"Yeah?"

"The *Indomitable* is moving." She pointed to the main screen, where they could see the lights of the cruiser's engines flaring.

Erik felt a moment of panic, before he calmed himself and examined the situation logically. The bow of the ship was still pointed away from Luna. It wouldn't make sense for the large ship to burn in that direction and then turn toward the moon, giving them more time to prepare for an attack. But he couldn't see any reason for the trajectory.

"What the hell are they doing now?"

TWENTY FIVE

He still remembered the day he got the call about his promotion and new posting. He'd been sitting in his shabby bachelor's quarters, watching a news program that was trying to convince people the Coalition was in more danger than it seemed. He had friends in Geneva who told him it was nothing more than overblown political posturing, though, and he believed them. Not that he liked it, since a war would do much to improve his chances of rapid advancement.

His last promotion, to lieutenant commander, had occurred four years earlier. More than enough time to have been given the next bump up the ladder. So long that he was beginning to think it was never going to come. After all, he was just some random nobody assigned to a backwater post in North America, where nothing important ever happened anymore. All the action was in Europe and Asia, where the main border between the Coalition and Syndicate split the continents.

When his tablet pinged with a communication request, he almost ignored it. He'd been off duty for an hour, and wasn't scheduled to go back on for another thirty five. The last thing he needed was to be called back in for some unimportant emergency that turned out to be overreaction by a poorly trained kid. His commitment to his job overruled that desire, however, and he groaned as he bent to stretch his arm out and grab the tablet.

The message displayed was a summons, but not immediate. The base commanding officer wanted him to report for a meeting at zero nine hundred the next morning. Dress uniform required. That made him curious and nervous at the same moment. Winters was tempted to start calling his friends on base, to see if anyone knew what might be going on. The CO would be upset if she found out, though, so he wisely resisted the temptation.

When he reported the next morning, he was fifteen minutes early and decked out in a freshly sanitized dress uniform. He only wore it a few times a year, when he was invited to important functions where the senior officers mingled with politicians and begged them not to reduce the military budget. It felt strange for him to be standing in the reception area with his ceremonial sword buckled around his waist, and his black boots polished to a shine that could blind someone if the sun hit them just right. The ensign working the desk didn't look twice, however, merely working on his display until he heard a buzz and signaled Winters to enter the office.

The base CO, a general in her late fifties who was known to be outspoken with unpopular opinions, was waiting for him. She returned his salute peremptorily, and then stood behind her desk. That was the first sign that something out of the ordinary was occurring; she would usually force people to stand looking down at her while she berated them or gave orders.

"Lieutenant Commander Benjamin Winters. It is my honor to inform you that you have been granted a promotion to the rank of Commander, effective immediately." She slid a leather case across the desk perfunctorily, and he grabbed it before it fell to the floor. Inside was the white rank pip that would replace the half black, half white pip next to two white ones on his chest. He was so amazed at the sight that he almost missed her next words. "You are hereby transferred to the Coalition Orbital Station, to take command there and serve a posting of at least six months. Your transport will leave this base at sixteen hundred hours. Any questions?"

Winters had tons of questions, starting with why him, but he knew from her tone of voice that the CO wasn't in the mood to answer any. He had the feeling she'd been pressured to promote him, and wondered for the first time if she had been the reason for his stagnant position since the last promotion. He limited himself to thanking her for the promotion, saluting crisply, and turning to leave the office.

His grin kept growing as he walked to his quarters, and his body felt like it was vibrating with his happiness. Finding a stack of boxes on his doorstep made him pause, but he didn't care why they were so eager to see him leave. He was glad to *be* leaving.

When he arrived on the station, he finally discovered the reason for his transfer. The previous commander had been colluding with the supply shuttle pilot, selling a portion of each shipment on the black market and then keeping the credits for themselves. It wasn't discovered until there was a medical emergency and the station's doctor couldn't find the meds that the inventory listed as having been delivered just a month earlier.

The crew on the station had been justly leery of him at first, trying to get a feel for what kind of leader he would be. The orbital station had become nothing more than a glorified surveillance post over the years, despite plans to turn it into a defensive weapons platform in the early days. When the Syndicate followed with their own station, the politicians had scrambled to get agreements in place that neither side would arm the stations. And so it remained a posting without much importance, a place where people ended up when they weren't good enough to be requested for a spot on a frigate.

Winters didn't care about any of that. He'd dreamed of being in space since he was a kid, watching news coverage of the domes on Luna being built. For six years straight, his birthday wish had been a trip to Luna, but his parents had never been wealthy enough to afford tickets on the daily transport shuttles. When he joined the Coalition Navy, he'd wanted to be posted to any frigate. He would have even been happy with a spot on the military cargo ships that ferried supplies from Earth to orbit. Instead, he spent twenty years being shuffled around bases on the planet until he had all but given up his dream of going to space.

His enthusiasm for the posting won over most of the crew, who grew to love working with their new commander. Winters was strict, but he also knew when to bend and let someone off with a warning if he found them contravening the regulations. They were far from Earth, staring down at the green and blue planet and reporting in to ground command once a day. It was the perfect place in his mind, where he could let his people be themselves and do their work the best way they knew how. As long as it all got done, and done well, he was content.

Watching the frigates leave the planet undefended had been his first uncomfortable moment. That was the first time since he'd arrived that he felt exposed and in some danger. It was a fear that was shared by many on the station, and Winters had to keep his calm exterior in place and reason with them that the odds were in their favor. Even if that behemoth of a ship arrived at Earth, surely some of the Coalition frigates would survive the encounter to provide protection.

When he was proved right, the crew on the station looked at him with additional approval in their eyes. He'd relished the feel of having their respect, beginning to wonder if he had been denied his true calling as a captain on one of those frigates. Captain Ben Winters had a fantastic ring to it.

The day the frigates exploded, raining debris on the planet below, Winters had been at his station in the command center. His chair was placed so he could look through the wall of windows, and they happened to be ideally placed to watch the destruction with silent shock. For a while, he'd worried that some of the debris might impact the station, but they got lucky and it all went wide of their orbital path.

From that day, things had been going steadily downhill. Half of his crew had been reassigned to the planet over a period of several days, leaving the station running long shifts with people responsible for multiple positions. The return of the *Waterloo* had given them a moment of hope, but then the ship went into orbit around Luna and Winters heard rumors from his friends on Earth that the admiral in charge had decided to back some pretender government instead of following orders from the true prime minister. He had wondered about that, until learning about the new Colonial Alliance. That was such an absurd concept that he dismissed any speculation that it could become a power in the system. He knew then that the so-called splinter government was no more than an attempt by Luna to forge legitimacy for themselves.

Admiral Holgerson had tried to contact him several times since then, but Winters refused the connection request each time. A new Fleet Admiral was in place on Earth, and he took his orders from the Admiralty. He would never turn his back on his own government, his own people.

It was a decision he never had cause to regret. Until he was woken with an urgent summons to the command center. "What's going on, lieutenant?" he asked as he floated through the upper deck door, still rubbing sleep from his eyes.

"Commander, the *Indomitable* has begun a burn. From our projections, they're going to pass very close to us."

Winters groaned, wondering why the Syndicate ship would want to do any such thing. Everyone knew the station wasn't a threat. They didn't even have flechette rifles on board, only a couple of old stun pistols that the security officers could access in emergencies. "Have there been any communications from the Admiralty?"

"No, sir. We received a warning from the *Waterloo*, though." Her voice was hopeful and inquisitive, and he knew she wondered how he would react to that.

"Thank the *Waterloo* for their concern," he said, dripping sarcasm. He wasn't going to work with a traitor, and a little bit of threatening posturing wouldn't change that. He pulled up the sensor logs on his display, charting the course of the cruiser. Her engines were running at low power, but still propelling the ship quickly toward the orbital station.

Winters put in a request for communication with the Admiralty, hoping they might have an idea of why the cruiser was suddenly moving after so long. And why it seemed to be on a collision course with his station. There wasn't time to try and slow their orbit, or speed past the point of the intersecting paths. Engines were another deficiency of the station; they only had small thrusters to help correct their course on rare occasions.

The trilling tones of a connection request continued to sound in his ear, but no one answered on Earth. Cursing, he stabbed the button that ended the request. Winters stared at the screen again, distressed to see the timer before collision continuing to drop precipitously. They had less than five minutes now, and the cruiser was still not deviating from their course. For a moment, he considered sounding the alarm to abandon the station, but he knew from drills that it would take too long to load the lifeboats and launch. There was a miniscule chance they might get out of the path of the Syndicate ship, but would be too damaged in the wake of the engines or by debris from the impact to survive a fall through the atmosphere.

As a last resort, Winters tapped buttons to contact the *Waterloo*. He sighed heavily, closing his eyes and sending a silent apology into the universe for not being good enough to save his people. When he heard the tone of an open channel, he opened his eyes again to see a stern woman's face. She was about his age. "This is Commander Winters, in charge of the orbital station."

"Commander Richtaus, XO," she said. "Winters, you need to abandon that station. Quickly!"

"It's too late for that," he said sadly. "I... well, I guess I just wanted to say that I should have spoken with you sooner. The Admiralty is refusing to answer my requests, and now I think I understand a small part of why you did what you did."

"Winters," a male voice said. A new face appeared on the screen, one that he recognized as Admiral Holgerson. "I'm sorry we can't do anything for you. We had no warning that this was going to happen."

"None of us did, sir." Winters cast his gaze over the command center he'd enjoyed working in for the last few months. He could see fear in the eyes of his lieutenant, and tried to give her a reassuring smile. "Promise me you'll make them pay for this."

Alarms began to blare, and Winters jerked his head around to see warnings appearing on the main displays. The cruiser had fired a torpedo, and it was moving fast. He had mere seconds left, and he again wondered why they would waste their time attacking an unarmed orbital station. Then he remembered the frigates under construction in the attached shipyard arm.

"We will remember," he heard Holgerson say. He barely had time to process the words before the world around him became light and fire.

Twenty Six

Erik couldn't believe what he was seeing. The *Indomitable* was passing through the debris cloud that had been the orbital station only minutes before. Unarmed and undefended, yet they slaughtered everyone on board without a second thought. Pulling himself together, he sent messages to the other freighters to pull them into formation.

"*Waterloo* is on channel four," Mira said.

He punched the button to pull up that channel on his holo display, and was met by the angry face of the XO. "Commander, I'm getting our ships into formation now. The *Viking* is minutes away from launching, but the *Tamerlane* is still half an hour from completion."

"Did you see what those bastards did?" Mags asked, her lips a tight line in a face white with rage. "They didn't even give them a warning, let them leave the station."

"We'll get revenge for those poor souls," Erik said. He turned his eyes to look through the holo display at the main screen at the front of the control room. "It looks like the *Indomitable* is changing course for Luna. They've increased power to the engines, as well. We have twenty seven minutes."

"It can't be soon enough," Mags said. "Admiral Holgerson wants your ships in formation as quickly as possible, and then we'll burn to meet them."

Erik nodded in response as the connection was closed. "You heard the woman, Mira. Get us into position." He flipped the switch for the ship's intercom system. "Everyone get to your station and strap in. It looks like the party is starting a bit sooner than we anticipated."

A chorus of voices let him know his crew was complying to the command, and he turned his attention back to the rest of the Alliance fleet. It took almost ten minutes to get them all into a rough line, and he reflected that they would need to add some training if the fleet survived the engagement. The freighter captains were too accustomed to following their own commands, and didn't react as quickly as they should.

The *Viking* slipped into her position to the right of the *Vagabond*, and Erik sent a message of greeting to the captain. It was good to see them, though the line had a hole on the other side that should have been occupied by the *Tamerlane*. They had six Alliance ships flanking the *Waterloo*, ready to meet the incoming cruiser.

"Report that we're in position and ready," Erik said, looking at the projections. The *Indomitable* was still speeding up, now only thirteen minutes out from intercept. He vowed that he wouldn't let the cruiser run away after a single quick volley of railguns and torpedoes, as they'd done against the Coalition fleet. This was all going to end here, today, no matter who came out on top.

Vegley was leaning over the rail, her body straining as if she could make the cruiser go faster with sheer willpower. Her cheeks were hurting from the wide smile on her face, pure unadulterated joy at being back in action at last. She wasn't sure she agreed with the admiral's decision to attack the orbital station first, or with his reasoning that he owed the Syndicate that much at the least. It had required little effort, but gave the frigate and freighters more time to prepare for them.

She could see those ships lined up now, seven of them turned to face the *Indomitable* head on. Vegley sneered at the arrogance of freighter captains thinking a few dinky light railguns could matter in a fight with a ship like hers. The cruiser would wipe them away as easily as she waved away an annoying pest buzzing in her ear.

The frigate was the only real threat, and it was such a small thing compared to the cruiser. Even in their reduced state, they still had twice the firepower of the *Waterloo*. They would tear the frigate apart, and leave the pieces behind as a monument to the folly of daring to oppose the obviously superior power.

"Commander," Yumata said in greeting when he joined her by the rail. They looked over the lively bridge, with officers rushing between stations as they prepared for the coming conflict. Despite the buzz of activity, she could detect an undercurrent of pleasant anticipation. She wasn't the only one on the ship who had been growing bored with the stagnant orbital patrol of the last few weeks.

"Everything is ready as ordered, sir. We have eleven functional railguns, one of the forward torpedo tubes is replaced and operational, and both rear tubes are still good to go."

"Superb work, commander. Please pass on my compliments to the crews who worked long hours to make sure we were as prepared as we could possibly be when this day came."

Vegley felt a flush of gratitude, reminded once again how well a good leader could inspire the people below them to work harder. It was a lesson someone should have taught Guildersen long ago, but she wondered if some people would ever be able to pick up on such a concept.

"Five minutes to targets," the weapons officer said behind them. The frigate and freighters were growing larger on the displays, and Vegley realized she was leaning forward again in eagerness. Her hands were sweating with nerves, her stomach was roiling with anticipation, and every part of her being longed for the thrill of battle.

The *Indomitable* was only minutes away when the doors to the side of the command deck hissed open. Fleet Admiral Holgerson stepped out of his office with a serene smile. To the crew and junior officers hurrying around, he would appear at ease. Mags had gotten to know the man well enough to see how tightly wound he was beneath the placid exterior. All of them felt anger and frustration at the loss of the orbital station, and the two frigates being constructed around it.

"Captain Andrews. Are we ready for engagement?"

"Ready and waiting at your order, admiral."

Holgerson stood at the rail, his eyes roaming the bridge below. He was apparently satisfied with what he saw, as he turned his gaze back to the Syndicate ship on the main displays. "Fire at will."

Mags immediately tapped the weapons officer on the shoulder, and the order passed down to the gun crews. Ten seconds later the first railgun rounds were propelled at incredible speeds. The tungsten rounds crossed the distance between the two warships in less than a minute, slamming into the hull of the massive cruiser and creating small plumes of debris. She was overjoyed to see the rounds firing at nearly twice the normal velocity. The reactor assist was giving them the power needed to punch deep into the enemy vessel.

"Torpedoes away," the weapons officer said. On the screens, dozens of tiny lights flared. Each torpedo was equipped with a small thruster to increase their speed. A low-level AI guided the missiles toward the intended target, ensuring the explosives were delivered as closely as possible to important sections of the cruiser.

A few people on the bridge cheered as explosions blossomed across the hull of the *Indomitable*. One of the explosions was massive, creating a large tear in the hull of the ship and exposing several decks to vacuum. Mags knew that it was little more than a mosquito bite to such an imposing ship. Another round of torpedoes was fired almost immediately, with the railguns never slowing their rate of fire that could expel three rounds every minute.

The cruiser finally returned fire, a hail of torpedoes shooting from the forward tube as railgun rounds began to impact the frigate. "Defensive turrets, take out those torpedoes!" an officer on the bridge called out urgently but calmly. The smaller guns were already firing, the AI tracking the incoming targets as quickly as their systems would allow.

Mags watched the screen as half the incoming missiles were destroyed, but braced for the impact of those that would slip through. A lieutenant was monitoring the damage control station nearby, calling out impact locations. "Decks seven and eight, port side, section B, hull damage and exposure to vacuum, seven confirmed dead. Deck nine, starboard, section L, minimal damage with no casualties…"

"Commander, the Alliance ships are advancing."

She joined the captain and admiral at the rail, watching on the large screens as the six freighters pressed forward.

"Take us in at a half G," Erik said, tapping the air to page through his holo display until he brought up the weapons menus. He'd only spent a short amount of time in the new system, and looked it over quickly to familiarize himself.

Outside of a few test firings during the last stages of the reactor tests, the heavy railguns attached to the *Vagabond*'s hull had never been used. With more power flowing through the magnetic coils and increasing acceleration of the tungsten rounds, he was hoping they would prove highly effective. He selected the button on the screen to commence the automated weapons program. The freighter shuddered as the first gun launched a fifty kilo round.

Tracking the individual shot was difficult amid the ordnance being fired by the frigate and other freighters, but he managed to keep his screen locked on the projectile until it impacted the cruiser amidships. "Woo!" he cried out joyfully. "We hit her!"

"Uh, cap, we've got torpedoes incoming."

Erik turned his attention to the missiles targeting his ship, cursing their lack of defensive weaponry.

The ship tilted sharply to the side as Mira threw the freighter into a roll. The chair restraints cut into his chest as they took the bulk of his weight.

On the screen he saw one torpedo overshoot the ship, but a second stayed in their wake.

"That torpedo is closing!"

"I'm working on it, cap." Mira sounded strained.

He was thrown back into the gel layer as she increased power to the ion engines, accelerating fast enough to stay ahead of the torpedo. On the large display covering the wall at the front of the room, the *Indomitable* grew larger as they rocketed toward it.

"Mira?"

The cruiser continued to grow on the screen, and he could make out hull plate seams as they got far closer than he'd ever hoped to be again.

"Mira!"

"No worries, cap," she assured him, half a second before throwing power into the ventral thrusters and pushing the *Vagabond* into a rising path. For a moment, Erik was afraid it was too little too late.

He closed his eyes and then forced one open in a tight squint to watch the view from the bow camera as they barely cleared the bumps and projections across the cruiser's hull. Small caliber rounds impacted the freighter, quiet pings sounding throughout the ship.

Behind them, the torpedo adjusted too slowly and slammed into the ship that had fired it.

"Hold on," Mira called out, as she kept the ship moving on a perfect arc. She cut the engines just as they flipped to face the cruiser again, this time accelerating away from it while the railguns fired as quickly as they could. Fifty kilo rounds were impacting around two targeted railgun emplacements on the Syndicate ship, destroying their ability to return fire on the *Waterloo*.

Fynn opened the ship-wide comm channel. "Erik, change targeting to the gun emplacements I'm sending over to your screen. I got a look at the others on our close pass, and they look to be disconnected. Probably repairs that haven't been completed yet, so they shoved some guns in there to look more dangerous than they are."

"That would explain the lack of return fire." Erik shifted their guns' focus, then typed in a quick message and sent it off to the frigate, hoping they'd already seen the same thing and were accounting for it in their targeting.

The other five freighters approached at that moment, following the Vagabond's lead and firing as quickly as their railguns would allow. The *Indomitable* had shifted their attention to the incoming ships, flinging rounds and torpedoes in their direction.

The first freighter got off a couple of shots, but then a bloom of fire engulfed the ship and sent it flying off on a tangential course. He hoped they were okay, quickly logged the ship for a check once the action was over.

By the time the others were firing at the Syndicate ship, the *Vagabond* was out of range and Mira was pushing the engines hard to reverse momentum and get them moving toward the cruiser again.

Erik was absorbed in watching the action, celebrating each hit his fellow Alliance ships scored. He was cheering on the *Montford*, a ship he'd enjoyed working with, when a railgun round found her fusion reactor and created a small sun in the midst of the battle. It was a brilliant explosion, purple-edged blue fire from the deuterium reactor that had just been installed.

"Shit," Mira said quietly, her attention riveted on the screen. The display had darkened to protect their eyes, and as it slowly returned to normal they could see that the explosion had taken out two other Alliance freighters. A large chunk was gouged out of the *Indomitable*, exposing more than a dozen decks to vacuum.

"Bring us in so we can fire into that hole," Erik said with a tight voice. He'd lost some great friends to the reactor detonation, and added their names to the long list of deaths that the Syndicate had to answer for.

Vegley raised a hand to the bump forming on the back of her head. She'd been thrown over the rail and into the main bridge below after the massive explosion. A brief thought of alarm passed through her as she wondered which parts of the ship had been damaged, but then she started to wonder which parts of herself had been damaged. She could feel a trickle of blood in her hair, and her left arm was starting to scream with agony where it had landed underneath her torso.

An ensign stumbled over to help her to her feet, and she winced as she saw how crooked her forearm looked under her uniform sleeve. A medical team was entering the bridge at that moment, but she knew others would need assistance more urgently than she did. Vegley held her arm against her stomach and waved away the orderly who was hurrying over.

She climbed the stairs to the command deck, having to stop halfway when a dizzy spell overwhelmed her. Panicked voices filled her ears, from above and below. Swallowing back the nausea that came along with the dizziness, she forced herself to continue up the stairs.

"Alliance ships are concentrating fire on our exposed sections!" the weapons officer cried out, looking around with wide eyes for someone to acknowledge the danger.

Vegley searched for Yumata, finding him laying in a heap against a wall. The communications officer was bent over him, and she felt the blood drain from her face at the thought that he could have been killed in the chaos. Without the admiral, she didn't know if she could hold the ship together.

A shower of sparks and a fresh jolt as the ship was shaken by another explosion brought her back to the moment. "Keep firing!" she cried hoarsely, pulling herself the rest of the way up the stairway. "Concentrate on that damned frigate!"

"No," a weak voice said. Vegley was relieved to see it was the admiral, being helped into a sitting position. "Get us out of here."

"Are you sure, sir? We can still win this fight."

"They have some kind of new weapons. We've done enough," Yumata said, his eyes closed in pain. A pair of medical orderlies hurried up the stairs, rushing over to look at him. He waved them away. "It's just a bump on the head. Look to those with more urgent injuries." His eyes fell on his XO, holding her injured arm protectively against herself.

As one of the orderlies checked on the other officers, the second approached Vegley and pulled her arm out to get a look. She gasped as a lightning bolt of pain shot through her arm, and again when her sleeve was forced up to show a broken bone pushing against the skin. She looked away as the medic administered a local anesthetic, ignoring his advice to report to the medical bay immediately.

Yumata was on his feet now, leaning heavily against a bulkhead as he directed the attempt at retreating from the battle. Vegley glanced at the damage control station, amazed at the size of the hole torn in the side of the cruiser. "What the hell did that?" she asked under her breath. The orderly looked up, but then turned his attention back to her arm.

Vegley felt her center of gravity shift as the *Indomitable* turned away from their previous course. She heard orders being passed through the bridge below, and people scrambling to lock down their stations before hurrying from the bridge. A glance over to the admiral showed him standing with a resigned slump to his shoulders, and an expression she had never seen on his face before. Defeat.

Mags was stunned by explosion, instinctively turning her eyes away from the screen even as it darkened to dim the brightness. The bridge fell quiet below, and the admiral sighed as the shock of it pushed the air from his body.

"Focus all fire on that!" Captain Andrews bellowed. She looked to see his outstretched arm pointing at a hole in the side of the cruiser. There were sparks of electricity around the ragged edges, bodies and debris floating into space. It was a huge cavity, creating a weak spot in the hull they could take advantage of.

Turning away from the main screens, Mags rushed to the weapons station and leaned against the back of the chair as the weapons officer changed the targeting focus. Tungsten rounds were fired through the hole, penetrating deep into the cruiser. She could see tiny fireballs appearing with many of the hits.

"The *Indomitable* is changing course," the sensor station called out.

"Are they returning to Earth?" Holgerson asked, turning from his place at the rail.

"No, admiral. Projections show they're moving onto a course for the outer system."

"Keep firing," the admiral said. He turned to Captain Andrews, speaking loudly enough that Mags could overhear. "We've done damage, but not nearly enough to cause them to flee. What is Yumata thinking?"

The cruiser turned its attention back onto the *Waterloo*, torpedoes and railgun rounds pouring in their direction. The sounds of impact filled the air, as the damage control station verbally listed each hit location. Casualties were mounting up quickly as the frigate turned to keep the Syndicate ship in her sights.

"Commander, the remaining Alliance ships are converging on the far side of the *Indomitable*. They continue to focus their fire on the section of compromised hull."

"Good, tell the *Vagabond* to give them hell." Mags paced behind the stations, her eyes roaming across the displays that showed the status of their own hull and the progress of the AI firing programs that were targeting the cruiser.

"Target the engines once they're in view," the admiral ordered.

"Yes, sir," she said, stopping at the weapons station to ensure the command was relayed through the targeting systems. The cruiser was picking up speed, and the *Waterloo* would soon be facing the rear of the large vessel. If they could take out one or two of the ion thrusters, they could slow the acceleration enough to keep pace and continue pumping rounds into it.

"Kestrels are launching." Mags heard the shout, but pushed it aside in her mind. The half dozen fighters they carried would try to place bombs along essential systems, but they were far too few in number to do much good against the Syndicate cruiser.

"Commander," the sensor station said urgently. She rushed over to look at the indicated display. "The *Indomitable*'s engines are overloading!"

"Recall the fighters," Captain Andrews yelled. "Get us away from that cruiser before it..."

The bridge was filled with a violent flash of light as the first of the behemoth's reactors exploded under the onslaught of fire from the frigate and freighters. The *Waterloo* shuddered under her feet, and Mags had to reach out to grip the nearest chair to prevent herself from being thrown to the deck. Her bioprosthetic arm had more than enough strength to keep her balance, and she reached out to steady those nearby.

Her ears were ringing from the overwhelming sound of the concussive shock wave hitting the frigate, and her balance was seesawing as she tried to stay on her feet. Mags knew there were people around her shouting in shock and pain, but her brain refused to process it. Her entire body felt numb, and she stared at the screen where the *Indomitable* had been only a minute before. The display was filled with an expanding cloud of debris, some almost as large as the frigate itself.

She fought against dizziness to pull herself along the row of stations, sliding into an empty seat. With shaking fingers, she tapped on the screen until the navigation controls appeared. The ship was in grave danger, and she knew she couldn't make herself heard to order someone else to get them out of it. Mags focused all of her willpower on the screen as she keyed in course changes. She sent the ship on a curving path out of the plane of the debris, adjusting course every time she saw some chunk of twisted metal and plastic intersect their path.

Mags didn't know how long she worked at the station, only that her vision was growing darker with every moment. Soon, the only thing she could see was the display. Her fingers were typing blindly, from long years of experience. The *Waterloo* was close to escaping the wreckage when she blinked and felt her body slump.

The last thing she registered before falling into unconsciousness was the muted blaring of a proximity alarm sounding through the bridge.

TWENTY SEVEN

Tuya was laying in her bunk, hands behind her head, staring up at the wooden slats of the bed only a few feet above. The room was growing dim as the light through the canvas walls faded. It was the end of her third day in the detainment camp, and boredom was killing her. There was nothing to do every day but sit around talking with the same people about the same things. The food was dull and never enough to do more than cut the hunger pangs for a short while.

She kept expecting the guards to drag her and Altan out to a shuttle to transfer them back to the *Indomitable*, but nothing had happened yet. She hoped that meant Guildersen had failed in his attempt to retake control. Or he forgot about them while thinking about his next meal instead. She could imagine that being a large part of his thought process every day.

Altan was snoring softly above her, his arm hanging over the edge of the bed with his fingers clenching and relaxing spasmodically as he dreamed. She laughed to herself, thinking of how the dog they'd had as kids would sometimes run in her sleep. Tuya couldn't resist the impulse, reaching up to lightly tickle her brother's palm until he snorted and pulled his arm back up onto his bed.

"It is good that you are together," Uju whispered from the bed beside her. "I do not have any brothers or sisters, but I imagine it is hard to be apart for so long."

"Yeah, it wasn't a fun time. Of course, thinking he was dead made it harder. If we'd been talking through video messages or whatnot, I would have at least had that minimum of contact."

They lay silently for a while, each lost in different thoughts. "What do you think it was?" Uju finally asked.

Tuya knew she was referencing the light show they'd witnessed the previous evening. It started with a bright flash in the sky to the northwest, visible even with the sun low in the sky nearby. The guards had let out whoops and hollers of joy as they watched flashes of meteors falling through the atmosphere. It took a while for word to get around that it had been the *Indomitable* destroying the Coalition's orbital station. She thought for sure it meant Guildersen had regained control, and was finally moving to wipe away any trace of Coalition presence beyond Earth.

Half an hour later, she'd seen people pointing up at the sky again. Twilight was deepening around them, and the sun had just dropped below the horizon. That made it easier to see the bursts of light that were appearing near the sliver of moon. Lights that flashed and faded quickly at first. But then there was a bright flash that made her think of a nuclear reactor exploding, though it seemed a larger explosion than she would have expected. Not long after was another bright flash, even larger than the first.

She had stared at the sky for hours after that as it became a deeper black speckled with stars. There was no information passed around this time about what they'd seen, only rumors that ranged from wild nonsense to plausible speculation. The consensus was that there had been a battle between the remnants of the two fleets, though few of the people in the camp could say how many ships each side had at this point. Tuya felt pretty sure the Syndicate was down to just the *Indomitable*, but didn't know what kind of strength the Coalition had left.

"I think it was the end of something," Tuya whispered. "I just hope it wasn't the end of all our hopes."

"We must always hold onto hope," Uju said firmly. "What else do we have if not hope?"

"You could be right. Hope has never been a specialty of mine. Too many years spent with my face shoved in the dirt every time I dared to hope for something. It didn't take long to realize that it was easier to expect nothing, so that I could never be disappointed."

A guard strolled by at that moment, causing them to fall silent. Whispered conversations were common amongst the hundreds of people who shared the building, but everyone quickly learned to stay silent when the guards were nearby. You only had to watch someone beaten once to understand what would happen if you were caught breaking the camp rules.

The man lingered near them, and Tuya watched through slitted eyes as he looked over the people lying on the beds with his night vision goggles. She knew that some of the guards like to stand around and watch the half naked women. Some detainees even woke to find one of their few pieces of clothing missing if they were foolish enough to take it off at night. Tuya hated the prison clothes she still wore, stiff and smelly with dirt and grime, but she would never take them off even to attempt washing them for fear that she might not get them back.

By the time the guard moved on, Uju was breathing softly and steadily. Tuya didn't want to wake the woman, so she rolled onto her side and folded her arms under her head.

She closed her eyes and tried to still her racing mind, but she couldn't stop thinking up escape scenarios. Almost all of them started with somehow wresting a gun away from one of the guards, and usually ended with a lot of bloody corpses strewn about as she led all the other detainees away from a burning camp.

She must have drifted off at some point, because the fantasies became more vivid. They also became crazier, with giant armored grunts marching at her side fighting off soldiers with red eyes and flaming swords. She was in the middle of one such dream when shouting and shots from flechette rifles jerked her eyes open.

Tuya sat up, banging her head against the slats of Altan's bed. Cursing and holding a hand against the top of her head, she swung her legs over the side of the bunk and blinked her eyes several times to get the sleep out of them. Her vision was still slightly blurry as she looked toward the canvas flaps at the end of the building. Shadowed figures were running across the opening, all seeming to be moving in the same direction.

Blinding light appeared overhead, flooding the canvas structure with illumination. Tuya twisted her head to look up as others around her began to groan and awaken. She could see indistinct lights, four or five at her best estimate, and they seemed to be getting closer. They were joined by another cluster of lights, and then a third.

She was on her feet by the time a fourth cluster of lights appeared, shaking Altan into wakefulness. Uju was already staring up with wide white eyes, and Tuya grabbed the woman's wrist to pull her up as Altan grumbled into wakefulness. "What?" he asked groggily.

"Something's happening outside," Tuya said, not bothering to keep her voice down. The noise outside the building was growing in intensity, and she didn't think the guards would be walking by to check on who was talking at that moment.

Altan finally lifted the arm that was covering his eyes, blinking in the bright light. "What the hell is that? Is it morning already?"

Tuya pulled on his sleeve until he rolled off the edge of the bed and dropped to his feet. "I'm thinking ships. The way the lights dropped from the sky, there are at least four of them. If they're shuttles to take us up to the *Indomitable*, I'm not waiting around for the invitation."

"Where could we go?" Uju asked, her focus still on the lights that seemed to be settling to ground level not far away. "I've seen a fence around the entire camp, and the guards have said more than once that it is electrified."

"We'll figure it out when we get there," Tuya said, pulling them along with her as she moved quickly for the far exit from the building. Normally there were guards flanking each doorway at all times, but she had a feeling they might have been drawn away by the commotion of the ships landing. There was still a lot of shouting and raised voices outside, and the occasional gun shot. It didn't sound like a friendly reception committee.

The group paused just inside the flaps, and Tuya turned to look back. She smiled tightly at Robbins, who had followed behind without a word, then nodded at him. Another set of hands might be useful if they found themselves in a scrape, even if she was still undecided on where his loyalties might ultimately lie. After all, he had been serving on the Syndicate cruiser for months before getting swept up in their transfer to the shuttle. Being left behind in the detainment camp must have been a real shock, though.

Tuya ducked her head through the opening, looking quickly in both directions. The guards were nowhere to be seen, as she'd expected. With a wave for the others to follow, she darted out onto the hard-packed dirt of the small area where the detainees could "exercise" for an hour each day; mostly they stood around in the open air, too packed into the space to do much else.

Three more canvas buildings surrounded the open ground, and she was glad to see no guards standing outside those doors. There were quite a few faces peering out from within the buildings, though. Detainees who weren't as brave as her small group, and wouldn't risk being caught where they shouldn't be.

One of the faces looking out locked eyes with Tuya. It was a young boy, pale and stick thin. His tiny arm lifted, finger pointing beyond her own building. She turned, unable to resist the curiosity against her instincts that were screaming at her to keep running. Those instincts quieted instantly when she saw the shape of four ships on the ground. Several of them looked familiar, one so much so that she'd know it no matter where she saw it.

"*Vagabond*," she said. Then she turned to the others, raising her voice so they could hear her over the commotion of increasing gun fire. "That's the *Vagabond*! These have to be Guild ships." Altan grinned at her, hope blossoming across his face once more. It made her happy to see her brother's optimism returning.

Shouting voices were approaching, and Tuya motioned for her group to run over and huddle beside the canvas wall of the nearest building. A handful of guards appeared moments later, faces shining with sweat and eyes wide with fear. They didn't even look back as they sprinted across the open ground, almost disappearing on the far side when three soldiers in ash gray armor over red biosuits appeared. The soldiers raised their rifles, firing calmly and efficiently. Tuya saw four of the guards fall, but one was able to escape.

The soldiers were spinning to return to the area around the ships, when one of them spotted the foursome. She lifted a fist to stop the others, and they all raised their rifles to point at the ground between them and the huddled group. "Step forward and state your name," the soldier barked.

Tuya felt Altan grab for her wrist, but she stood and raised her hands to show she was unarmed. She stepped forward into better light so the soldiers could see that she wasn't dressed like one of the camp guards. "I'm Tuya Sansar. This is my brother Altan, and two fellow detainees."

"Philip Robbins," he said, stepping forward to stand beside Tuya.

"Uju Tyjani." The woman joined them, her hands also raised at shoulder level.

The soldiers talked between themselves quietly, their weapons relaxing to point nowhere in particular. Altan leaned close, whispering in her ear. "That symbol on their chest. That's the *Telemachus* logo." Tuya examined the symbol, a hand pulling back an arrow nocked to a bow, recognizing it from the long ago days when she would trade video messages with him while he served on the freighter.

"Wait here," the female soldier said. "The captain is on his way."

"Which captain?" Tuya asked, thinking of the four ships. The soldiers didn't answer, though. Two of them jogged away, heading back toward the ships, while the other two remained standing a few meters away. More people were poking their heads out of the canvas buildings now, looking with curiosity at the soldiers in armor they'd never seen before.

Footsteps alerted her to someone approaching at a jog, and then a man appeared from behind the building. There were two stars painted in the center of his chest plate, one fully red and the other half gray. Tuya thought they might be rank designations, but she had no idea what they could signify. He approached the soldiers, spoke a few quiet words, and then turned to face her group as the guards left the area.

"Tom!" Altan said, stepping forward with a wide grin on his face.

The soldier nodded, reaching up to remove his helmet. Tuya recognized his face, one of the men who'd been part of the escape from the *Indomitable*. He was grinning just as widely at them. "Altan, it's so good to see you. We were worried they might have killed you on that ship."

"What's going on? Who are those soldiers, and what armor are you wearing?"

Tom snorted, shaking his head. "That is a long story, old friend. Short version is that we're with the Alliance, and here specifically for you two."

"Alliance?" Altan asked, sharing a confused look with her.

Another person appeared from around the building, running over to join them. "Did they find them?" His blue eyes locked on the group of detainees, and he rushed over to wrap her in a tight hug. "Tuya!"

She hugged him back, surprised to feel a swell of emotion overtake her. Tears started to fall as she buried her face against the chest of the captain who had become as close as family. "Erik! How did you find us?"

"Not everyone down here agrees with the way things are going. One of our informants told us about this place, and sent us a video showing most of the detainees. As soon as I heard about it, I knew we had to get you back."

"We need to wrap up the reunion," Tom said, pulling his helmet back on. They could hear rifles firing close by. "Not all of those guards are afraid to fight, and we're outnumbered."

Tuya released her old captain, following as he and Tom led them away from the small exercise yard. She looked back to see pale faces still staring out at her from inside the buildings. A few people had grown brave enough to step just outside the flaps, but no more than a step. She felt a tug at her heart, looking at them. "What about all these other people? We have to do something for them, Frost."

He shook his head, lips tight and eyes hard. "If it were up to me, we'd take as many as we could. But Meyers and Brighton are against it. Political complications."

"Political complications?" Tuya felt her anger growing, fueled by the pathetic faces looking at them as they passed another opening. "We're going to leave these poor people behind because of politics?"

Erik sighed, but nodded. "Things have changed a lot, Tuya. Especially in the last few days." He wouldn't say anything more as they approached the ships sitting on the ground. *Vagabond* was the closest, the ship scarred and gouged as if it had been in a heavy battle recently. The doors at the nose of the ship were open, the ramp extended. Half a dozen of the soldiers in gray and red flanked it, protecting the ship as Erik led the group up the ramp. Two people were waiting at the top, smiling in welcome. "Fynn, Jen, get these guys settled in. Tom, get your Marines loaded up and we'll blow this rock."

Tom raised a hand in a brief salute, turning away to speak into his helmet comms. Tuya was wrapped in another hug as the old engineer greeted her, and she could see Altan and Jen sharing one, as well. She still didn't feel right about leaving the other detainees behind.

A cough drew her attention back to Robbins and Uju, standing uncomfortably amid people they didn't know. Tuya introduced them to Fynn and Jen, as they were led deeper into the ship to get strapped in at open stations in the medical bay.

"Excuse me," Uju said. "Did I hear your captain mention Mr. Brighton? Would that be Rinde Brighton?"

"Yes," Jen replied. "Do you know him?"

"I worked for him for many years." Uju looked down at the ground, and Tuya knew she was feeling shame at how that had ended. She reached out to squeeze the woman's hand in support. "He is safe?"

"He's on Luna," Fynn told her as they entered the med bay. "Prime Minister of a splinter government, set against the corrupt administration here on Earth." The old engineer snorted with disgust. "The same administration that totally capitulated yesterday, surrendering all territories to the Syndicate."

"What?" Tuya and Uju both asked in shock. Altan's eyebrows were raised, but he didn't seem as surprised by the development. Robbins groaned in despair as he was strapped into a crash couch. She wondered if he regretted joining their escape now.

"You have a lot to catch up on," Jen told them. They heard the clunk of the cargo bay doors closing, and then Erik spoke over the intercom to tell everyone they needed to be strapped in.

"We're taking rifle fire from the guards. It's not enough to damage the hull, but I don't want to give them too many opportunities for a lucky hit that could take out our thrusters. Hold tight, folks."

Tuya wrapped her hands around the restraints over her chest. She felt a surge of joy as the ship shuddered and lifted from the ground. After a few seconds, she felt the vibration of the engines as the main thrusters fired to push them away from Earth. It felt different than she was accustomed to, as if the ship were moving faster, but she put it down to almost a year away from the freighter. She didn't much care. They were leaving Earth, going back to Luna where she knew she could fall back into her old life.

TWENTY EIGHT

Meyers slumped over his desk, head in his hand as he looked over his display. "They got them. That's some good news, at least."

Rinde Brighton was sitting on the other side, and he breathed a sigh of relief at the words. "I am glad to hear it, my friend. We need something good to hold up our spirits."

"There's more," Meyers said, raising his head to look at Brighton. "There are two others with the Sansars. I'm not sure who this man Robbins is, but I believe you might know the other. Uju Tyjani."

Brighton sat forward eagerly. "Uju is safe? My heart is full of joy to hear that."

"You don't hold a grudge? She's the one who betrayed you to the prime minister, after all."

"No. Uju did only what she knew was necessary. Knowing what we do, I am certain they threatened more than just her job. They probably threatened her family, her mother back in Lagos."

Meyers nodded, convinced that such a thing was probably behind the betrayal. If he had been in the other man's position, facing the return of Dex after she worked against him, he hoped he would be as forgiving. Especially in light of all the other losses they had sustained over the last few days.

Three freighters had been lost in the battle against the *Indomitable*. A large chunk of their already diminished fleet, leaving them woefully short of ships. When the four he had dispatched to collect representatives from the mining colonies returned, they would need to be armed to join the defense of Luna.

The *Waterloo* had also suffered a great deal of damage. The frigate was still intact, but half the crew had been killed during the fight. The bridge itself had been obliterated when the ship flew through the debris field left by the destruction of the cruiser. In the space of seconds, the Coalition's last ship had lost all senior officers and staff. Repairs would be started as soon as they could find a place to land it on Luna's surface, but it would be months before it was space-worthy again.

The threat of the *Indomitable* being gone was cause for celebration, but Meyers and Brighton had been unable to join the festivity. Too many people had been lost, too much damage done to their hopes for the future. The Syndicate orbital station was all that remained of Earth's control beyond the planet's atmosphere. If nothing else, the Colonial Alliance was more of a reality than it had been a few days earlier.

With the Coalition surrender to the Syndicate, a severe blow had been dealt to Rinde's hope of reaching the planet to sweep the corrupt administration out before it was too late. There were still pockets of resistance, soldiers and citizens who didn't want to lose their freedoms, but already more and more people were accepting the change with apathetic shrugs. It baffled Meyers to think how easily such a large population could be swayed.

A ping from his display drew his attention, where he found a message waiting from Dex. "The *Vagabond* is on approach. We should go meet them." Brighton nodded, rising to his feet to follow Meyers from the office. As they walked through the Hall, he noticed the renewed vitality of all the people working at the desks that were stuffed into the space. They knew only that the Alliance had won the fight, without factoring in the costs of that victory.

It was the same on the streets of Aldrin, where the two men were met with smiles and joyful greetings. The citizens of the dome had lived for so long with the threat of the cruiser hanging over their heads on top of the bombings that had killed so many. Meyers couldn't blame them for feeling happy and free now that it was gone.

The dome looked different to him these days. Many homes and businesses had the Colonial Alliance flag hanging from windows, showing their support for the new government that was building laws and procedures for the expansion of humanity beyond their homeworld. It was an expansion that had become all but dormant, ignored in the ongoing cold war between the governments on Earth that had claimed dominion over the entire system.

Meyers hoped that with the Alliance in charge now, they could push farther out into the system. It would take years, however, to rebuild what had been lost in the recent battles. They would also have to work hard to increase the populations of the colonies, and even Luna itself. His own dream was the construction of a third dome, larger than Aldrin and Armstrong combined, to further expand their capacity. Luna was hard pressed to sustain the almost three thousand people now stuffed into the two domes.

When they reached the docking facility, Dex was waiting for them just inside the entry. Meyers chuckled, seeing how her attention was focused so strongly on the airlock the *Vagabond* would be using. It was going to be the first time she saw Frost since he left to prepare for the confrontation with the Syndicate cruiser. Meyers had shared the information about Tuya Sansar as soon as the battle was complete and the ships had done all they could to stabilize each other. It had taken every ounce of persuasiveness to keep the determined young captain from rushing off at that moment to rescue her alone, instead of waiting for a group of freighters and cargo shuttles to be organized with Alliance Marines onboard to fight off the Syndicate guards.

Meyers hated himself for not being able to save everyone else held in the camp, but he and Brighton had agreed that the domes couldn't sustain additional people. Without the infrastructure to support them, bringing the detainees here would do nothing but condemn them all to a slow, spiraling death. He had to hope that thinning out the guards would give the people in the camp the ability to stage an escape on their own.

He and Brighton stood straighter as the airlock began making noises indicating the outer door was opening for people to enter. Erik Frost wasn't alone as he stepped out of the airlock. He was followed by four people who looked ragged, filthy, and exhausted despite the smiles on most of their faces.

"Uju!" Rinde cried out, rushing forward to greet his former aide. The woman looked hesitant about what kind of reception she might get, but Rinde was smiling widely and laughing with joy. Soon, both of them were laughing and crying as they hugged.

Erik glanced at the reunion with a half-smile, leading another man and woman forward. "President Meyers, this is Tuya Sansar, the member of my crew who stayed behind on

Indomitable. And this is the brother she stayed to rescue, Altan Sansar."

Meyers stepped forward to shake hands with both of them, greeting them warmly and welcoming them back to Luna. "Mr. Sansar, you may find it hard to believe, but I remember meeting you back when you served on the *Telemachus.* Oh, I wasn't the Guild president back then, just a representative dealing in higher value cargo. I saw your crew in a bar one night, and your captain invited me to join you."

Altan's brows were furrowed as he tried to work up the memory, and finally his eyes brightened. "I remember! Captain Jones told us that you were going places, and he had to brown-nose while he could." He was smiling with the words.

Meyers laughed, nodding. "Yes, that is Captain Jones in a nutshell. We all took it very hard when his ship was lost, with all of you never coming back. And yet, here you are. Four of you have returned to us, and we are thankful for it." He turned his attention to the last of the detainees, a man in his thirties who was staring around at the docking facility and frowning. "Who's this?"

Erik shrugged, waving the man forward. "This is Specialist Philip Robbins. He was a member of the Engineering crew aboard the *Indomitable* who happened to be sleeping off a bit of a bender when Altan managed to insert transfer orders into the system. Once the group was found by Syndicate soldiers, he was left behind in the detainment camp."

"Ah," Meyers said, reaching out to shake the man's hand. "I am sorry to hear you were abandoned in such a way, but I assure you it was a better result than still being aboard the cruiser."

"Yeah." Robbins looked sad, but resigned. "I don't think I ever really fit in there, anyway. The whole reason I always got drunk was because there was nothing else to do between shifts."

Meyers examined him, wondering how far he could be trusted. At the same time, it sounded as if the man had skills that could be very useful to the Alliance. "Are you looking for transit to Earth if we can ever arrange that, Mr. Robbins? Or would you like to stay here and work with us? I'm sure we can find several jobs for a man with your skills."

Robbins looked surprised at that. "You, uh, don't mind that I'm technically the enemy?"

"Sir, no one man or woman is our enemy. Just the institution as a whole. If you're willing to work with us, then I'm more than willing to work with you."

"Well.. then I accept." Robbins still looked amazed at the offer, as if he'd been expecting to be tossed into a cell instead. Meyers passed him off to Dex, asking her to show him back to the Alliance Hall where he could be assigned lodging and a job. The engineering teams working to increase the effectiveness of the dome systems to handle the larger population would be appreciative of another skilled hand.

Meyers turned back to Erik and the Sansars. "Now, let's get the two of you into a room so you can clean up. I'm sure we can find some better clothing for you, and then we'll all meet and figure out what to do with you."

"I've already offered them positions on my crew," Erik said, tucking his thumbs under his belt. "I don't know if we'll have much need for cargo specialists, but we do need weapons technicians and I trust Tuya and Altan much more than some newbie off the street."

"Excellent! It's good to see crew come home."

Rinde and Uju joined them, still smiling and wiping away happy tears. "Uju has agreed to come back to work with me." With the Coalition agreeing to be absorbed into the Syndicate, the splinter government on Luna had voted unanimously to join the Alliance. Rinde was elected as the representative of Armstrong dome, filled with the people taken from the factory where political dissidents and agitators had been sent. They still had dreams of getting back to Earth to re-establish a democratic government there, but Meyers knew it could be a long time before their forces were ready for such a move. The Syndicate had already started taking control of land-based missile and defensive systems, ready to fight off any attempt at landing troops to help the now rebel forces.

Captain Frost and the Sansars retreated through the airlock to return to *Vagabond*, where the siblings could settle into their new quarters and get cleaned up before the entire crew reentered Luna for a ceremony to reward the brave captains and crews who put their lives on the lines for the citizens of the Alliance.

TWENTY NINE

Erik ran his hand along the cool metal of the railing, admiring the workmanship that had gone into the construction of the new command deck. The bridge below was almost completed, with technicians still working to install consoles and terminals for the crew who would fill the seats. It had taken three months, but the frigate was finally close to being fully repaired. They'd even managed to salvage some railguns from freighters that were too badly damaged to ever be used again, to fill holes on the frigate where weapons had been destroyed in the battle.

During the construction, they had improved on the connections with the fusion reactor. It was now tied into all weapons systems, and even a new defensive shield that Amelia thought would at least slow any rounds fired at the ship, limiting the damage they could do. At the same time, a second reactor was added in a separate location, providing backup in the event of issues or damage to one of them. Both were significantly shielded, making it harder for a lucky shot to cause an explosive failure.

The ship was going to be the new flagship of the Colonial Alliance, and Meyers was already working to set aside funds for the construction of another frigate. With five asteroid colonies, two moons, and a planet to protect, they wanted to be sure a ship was ready to rush to anyone's aid at a moment's notice. In the future, ships would patrol the asteroid belt, and even push into the outer system for scientific studies and eventual colonization of moons around Saturn and Jupiter.

Standing there, Erik could see it all stretching before him. He hoped much of it would happen during his lifetime. He especially hoped he would have the opportunity to see new planets and moons close up. It surprised him how much he yearned for the chance to stand on this very spot and look at the eye of Jupiter's storm or the rings of Saturn looming large on the displays wrapping around the bridge.

Fynn and Amelia were already ensconced in Engineering, taking over the running of the ship's engines. Ensign Graves was still in charge of the department, but he welcomed the experience of the other two and accepted their input on even the smallest tasks.

Isaac had carved out a spot among the frigate's technicians, and was enjoying the challenge of building new programs to work with larger systems. Erik had been convinced to keep the frigate's AI, with the condition that Isaac agreed never to tinker with it to try improving its intelligence levels.

Jen was working beside the medical staff still on board, and had told Erik how much she enjoyed being able to put her skills and training to use on a daily basis. There were only about a hundred people on the ship at the moment, but the full crew complement would be three times that number.

Mira was overseeing work on the bridge below, making sure everything was set up just right. She'd be stationed on the command deck when the ship was operational, where Erik had put her in charge of the navigational and piloting stations. He'd caught her talking quietly to the ship a few times already, and felt reassured that she would handle the change well.

The *Vagabond* had been passed on to a new captain and crew. Leaving the ship he grew up on had been hard, but Erik recognized the importance of moving into the frigate. As head of the growing Alliance fleet, he needed to command from the deck of the most powerful ship. He still kept an eye on his old ship, offering advice now and then to the young woman who was commanding a ship for the first time.

The doors onto the command deck swished open almost silently, and his wife entered to join him at the rail. It had been a small ceremony the week before, with only their closest friends in attendance, and he still couldn't stop grinning every time he saw Dex and thought of her as his wife.

"She's looking fantastic, isn't she?" he asked, marveling at the clean lines and immaculate detail work at the stations on the command deck.

"Absolutely beautiful," Dex replied, her eyes locked on his face. She was smiling, but it was a wistful and sad smile. He knew she was thinking that once the frigate was completed he would be leaving her again for another trip off Luna.

"I've been thinking." He paused, turning to look down into her shining amber eyes. "We were going to keep her name, to honor all those who died fighting against the *Indomitable*. But I think she needs a new one, to let people know the Alliance is here to stay."

"What name would you give her?"

Erik smiled. "I was thinking *Resolute*."

ACKNOWLEDGEMENTS

This series has been a real labor of love for me. For so many years, I never thought I'd actually be able to put the stories in my head onto paper. I hope everyone reading this has enjoyed the series. (Just between you and me, I have so much left to write about Erik Frost and the crew of the *Vagabond*. I hope to have the chance to continue their story one day if the sales justify it.)

I also want to thank my friend Jessica. She always gives me great feedback on my writing, and has been an occasional sounding board for my projects.

About The Author

Tim has been a dreamer since he was a small boy, and is finally putting all his wild imaginings onto paper. During the day, he is an IT support technician for a nationwide bank. At night, he bangs away on his keyboard and often obsesses over the proper word to express an idea or feeling.

He can be found online at www.timrangnow.com, where you can sign up for a monthly newsletter to get all the latest updates on current projects, exclusive access to short stories set in the Guild universe, and advance peeks at future books.

Vagabond

Indomitable

Waterloo

Resolute

www.ingramcontent.com/pod-product-compliance
Lightning Source LLC
Chambersburg PA
CBHW060425180626
46817CB00007B/2676